10/16

Once, in a Town Called Moth

Trilby Kent

Tundra Books

Tundra Books, a division of Random House of Canada Limited,
a Penguin Random House Company

Library and Archives Canada Cataloguing in Publication

Kent, Trilby, author
   Once, in a town called Moth / Trilby Kent.

ISBN 978-1-101-91811-1 (bound)

   I. Title.

PS8571.E644O53 2016   jC813'.54   C2015-905759-0

Published simultaneously in the United States of America by Tundra Books of Northern New York, a division of Random House of Canada Limited, a Penguin Random House Company

Library of Congress Control Number: 2015955120

Edited by Samantha Swenson
Designed by Leah Springate
Jacket image: (braid) © Christy Elle Photography/Getty Images;
(quilt) Tammy Venable/Shutterstock
Printed and bound in the USA

www.penguinrandomhouse.ca

1 2 3 4 5   20 19 18 17 16

Penguin Random House
TUNDRA BOOKS

for Clea

. . . I know
With the dawn
That you will be gone,
But tonight you belong to me

Yesterday, we left Colony Felicidad for good. Left Justina and the chickens and the boys' dungarees hanging from the clothesline. Left the little girls playing under the *tipu* tree. Left Susanna wrapping tortillas in paper in the bakery, listening to the ticking of the frozen clock that only counts the seconds between 1:42 and 1:43. Left the dogs scratching in the sun, snapping at flies. Left the rows of slate tablets in the schoolhouse, left the cows staring mournfully beyond the wire fence, left Agustín in his pickup loaded with barrels of diesel.

We are at the airport in Santa Cruz now, Papa and I, and tomorrow we will be in Canada.

I still don't know why.

Toronto

THE HOUSE WAS SMALL: a clapboard box on a square, weed-strewn lot fringed by a green wire fence. The owner was an elderly Italian woman called Mrs. Fratelli who lived on the other side of town in Little Portugal. Ana didn't know how her father had found Mrs. Fratelli or the house; she only knew that the rent was cheap and that he paid half of it in kind, by rebuilding the front porch and traveling across town a few times a week to do odd jobs for Mrs. Fratelli and her neighbors.

The neighborhood was not quite as shabby as the house. It was what people in these Canadian cities described as "up and coming." Children played in front gardens, old men smoked and read the newspaper in camping chairs, and fancy cars sometimes got keyed at night. Ana had never seen so many houses so close together. Why, in this enormous country, did they have to huddle against each other like this, as though space was running out? Perhaps for warmth: the winters here were cold, she knew.

Inside, the house was dark in shades of brown and yellow. Yellow linoleum in the kitchen, brown trim in the front room. A narrow staircase with a stained beige carpet fraying on the sides. Upstairs, a bathroom with a shower and toilet with a permanent brown stain seeping down the pipe. Two bedrooms: her father's at the back, with a bed and built-in closet (only one of the doors opened); Ana's room had just enough space for a single bed and a nightstand with a mirror, but it looked out onto the street and got the most light in the entire house.

There was little furniture. The two beds and nightstand, a table and four folding chairs in the kitchen, and a squashed, faded sofa in the front room. There was a barbecue lid on the back porch, but no barbecue. A broom but no dustpan. A few mugs in the kitchen cup-board—one white with a cartoon dog and SNOOPY written in bubble letters; two blue pottery ones with brown speckles in the glaze that looked like mold—and a pack of paper plates. That was it.

"Stay inside, and don't answer the door to anybody," Papa said on the first day, as he went out to buy food. So Ana had sat on her bed and looked out the window at the street, where people walked dogs and children rode scooters and cars parked and locked and pulled away again.

By the third day, Papa had drawn Ana a map of the neighborhood. There was a supermarket a few blocks away, and a pay phone on the corner for emergencies. "It's safe," he told her. "You need fresh air and sun and exercise. Don't talk to anyone, though, and stay within these four streets."

By the second week, she was going out every day, walking up and down the two streets running parallel to their own and tracing the perimeter up to Danforth Avenue and back down to the park. She wandered the aisles in the supermarket and stood in front of the freezer to cool down when the humidity outside got too much.

"If anyone asks, remember that you're Ana now," her father said. "Not Anneli."

He had given her sweatpants to wear at the airport and bought jeans for himself. Her dress and his overalls were bundled into a plastic bag and left at the bottom of the wardrobe.

"When Mrs. Fratelli pays me, I'll buy us some good clothes," he said. "Don't worry."

Colony Felicidad

When I was little, sometimes I'd narrate what I was doing as if I were a character in a book: *Anneli is making breakfast. She breaks an egg into the frying pan, and then she remembers that the butter needs to be taken out. The slap of a jump rope hitting the dusty ground means that Eva is playing behind their house. Anneli remembers the frying pan and lifts a fork from the drawer . . .*

Thinking about myself like that meant the story could change. Anneli could change. The past, and the present . . . and the future too.

But, of course, it was just a game. I liked it that way.

———

I once asked Susanna where she would have grown up if her grandparents hadn't lived in a colony, and if they hadn't left Canada to start a new life with other Mennonites in Bolivia.

"In a city," I said. "Which city would they have gone to?"

"They wouldn't have. They only knew what it was like to live on a farm."

"I know, but *if*. What was the nearest city?"

Susanna paused in her kneading, her hands ghostly with flour, and pushed a strand of hair from her face with one shoulder.

"Edmonton," she said.

"Where's that?"

"North of Calgary. It's on a river."

"So, just like here."

"I don't think so."

"Do you ever wish you'd grown up there instead?" I asked her.

"What difference would it make?"

"It would change everything."

"But I wouldn't know that. Neither would you."

That last bit was meant to shut me up, and it did. Sometimes it's just not worth trying to get someone else to wonder about the things you do. Susanna had enough on her mind, what with her sister being pregnant and no one else knowing.

"Maria will start showing soon," I said. "What's she going to do then?"

Susanna slapped the dough hard upon the table.

"That's not for you to worry about, Anneli," she said. "It's not your life."

Toronto

ON THE DAYS WHEN he wasn't working for Mrs. Fratelli, Ana's father went out with a pocketful of quarters for the pay phone by the bus stop. Ana didn't know who he called. Sometimes he was only gone for a few minutes; other times, an hour or more. She tried not to think about what it would mean if he never came back.

One afternoon, a few seconds after she heard the front door close, he came up to her room and placed a plastic bag on her bed.

"I wasn't sure of your size," he said. He took out six cans of Jumbo Beef Chili and a pack of toilet paper and nudged what remained in the bag toward her. "There should be enough to see you through the next little while. We can always go back once we're a bit more settled."

She waited until he'd left before pulling out the clothes folded haphazardly inside the bag, which had the words EXPRESS PHARMA-CARE printed in red letters on it. It should have been funny, interpreting his attempts at a normal teenage wardrobe only with a modesty factor of one hundred. There were a pair of blue jeans, baggy and shapeless, and two sweatshirts (*Camp Kawinpasset '96* said one; *Miller's U-Haul* said the other). Beneath these, a white button-up collar shirt with green paisley-patterned stripes. Two turtlenecks: one pink, one purple. A pair of black, Velcro shoes. A three-pack of socks that Ana could already tell were too small. The clothes didn't look new—he must have bought them secondhand.

The jeans fit better than she'd expected. Even though she had to roll the cuffs—she was tall, but not *that* tall—and would need a belt to keep them from gaping at the back, they could have been worse. The denim felt hard and heavy around her legs, like a cast, and made a starchy noise when she walked. The purple turtleneck clung to her waist and chest, but that didn't matter: no one would see it under the

Camp Kawinpasset sweatshirt. The shoes fit and were comfortable. Ana unrolled the cuffs of her jeans so that they covered the Velcro straps. Then she stood on the bed and regarded herself in the dressing table mirror.

At least it's less obvious than the dress.

Her father looked up as she entered the kitchen. "Well," he said. "Well."

"I thought I'd go for a walk."

"Dinner will be ready soon." He looked her up and down again. "Don't talk to strangers."

I don't know anyone here, she thought. *Everyone's a stranger. You might as well say, "Don't talk to anyone."*

Instead she said, "I'll just be five minutes. To the end of the street and back."

—#—

The sky was the color of sour milk, streaked with airplane trails, crosshatched with telephone wires and streetcar lines. It was as if someone had stretched an enormous sheet of chicken wire overhead.

There were hardly any people on the street, and yet there was noise. The distant growl of a highway, the hum of idling cars on the main strip, the creak and sigh of tree branches, the squawking laughter of children playing, unseen, in a laneway between the houses. The houses were lined up close, closing the gaps between them with gates and fences like clasped hands.

Ana stood at the corner feeling that she should want to cross the road. Something stopped her. She thought of her father back in the kitchen, imagined him opening the front door and walking off down the street in the other direction, away from her, untraceable. Her heart thrummed. Instinctively, she turned and swiftly retraced her steps.

He was still in the kitchen when she returned, and she felt her entire body slacken with relief.

"That was quick," he said.

How am I to be today?

It depended on her father's mood. That much, at least, hadn't changed. Most days, it was easiest to be invisible. Neutral. Cook, clean, pray. To make it more interesting, she would pretend to be a housewife, a mother with responsibilities. A make-believe life. But then there were mornings when her father's eyes glittered with mischief under that heavy, glooming brow. On those days, she could be more free: loving, lively. She could ask questions.

"Why are we here?"

Her father didn't turn around. From somewhere behind those broad, hunched shoulders, she heard him say, "To see her again."

"Who?" A foolish question, which he ignored. "Why here, though? Why not her cousin's farm? Where there are other people like us."

"Because she's not on the farm. I've contacted them already. She's probably here."

"How do you know?"

"I know." When he turned around again, the sparkle had left his eyes: they were dark, like the reflection of drifting clouds in pond water.

"When will we see her?"

"Soon."

The next time she asked, again he said, "Soon."

After the third time, Ana stopped asking him. Instead, the question turned outward: past her, past them, past the house and the street. Silently interrogating every stranger she passed on the sidewalk, every shopper waiting in line, every averted gaze at the bus stop.

When will I see you? When?

And how will I know?

Help me to see her. Open my eyes so that I'll recognize her.
Open his heart so that he'll forgive her.
Please. Please. Please.

———※———

When they had finished the six cans of Jumbo Beef Chili, Ana asked her father if she could buy provisions for the next week.

"We have fifteen dollars," he told her.

No treats, he meant. He could have eaten Jumbo Beef Chili for a month. One night he had brought home a cardboard box with hot grease stains seeping through the bottom, and they had eaten a circle of soggy bread covered in melted cheese and a red paste. Another night he had brought home dinner for two in a plastic container, only for Ana to realize that it was just half cooked and needed a machine they didn't have to heat it through. In the end she had dumped it all into a pot and warmed it on the stove top, with moderate success. But she had begun to crave apples, peas and cucumbers. Avocado. The crunch of lettuce or even cabbage.

There was a supermarket down the main road, past the convenience store where her father had found the tins of Jumbo Beef Chili, past a playground and a garage and a row of stores with faded clapboard signage. Ana listened to the cars as she walked, trying to distinguish the ones that would come rumbling past her from the ones that roared up and down the main road. Buses sounded different: the rhythmic rumble and screech as they slowed down, the clatter of doors opening and clapping shut, the beeping of a wheelchair ramp being lowered. All of these noises were new to her. Streetcars spoke with a low metallic hum, a bell like the one on Isaac's bike back home.

In Bolivian cities, the traffic could be overwhelming, too: the cars overstuffed and falling apart, belching fumes, the roads shared with bicycles and wagons and pedestrians and sometimes livestock. Noisy, pungent chaos. Here, what startled Ana more was the efficiency of it all: the markings on the road, the coordinated streetlights. She had watched several cars come to a four-way stop and take turns, one by one, to make the crossing. *Is that normal?* she'd found herself wondering. *Is there a code for who gets to go first?* The noise and motion seemed choreographed in a way that could only be possible if everyone followed the same rules. But how did they know the rules in the first place?

Inside the store, the linoleum was scratched and the dingy lights gave everything a yellow cast. Ana rummaged through a large wire bin filled with boxes dotted with red REDUCED stickers and wondered how angry her father would be if she brought home a pack of Twinkies.

She dropped a head of broccoli into the basket; some carrots, two tomatoes. There was a small, dark lettuce on the shelf next to the prepared salads labeled *bok choy*; she sniffed it, pressed the leaves between her fingers, put it back.

Eggs, potatoes, a can of corn, an onion. That would do for a pot of soup. She found some chicken that had been reduced to two dollars; the boneless meat had squashed down into a corner of the container, pooling red juice. If they were careful, they could eat reasonably well for three, four days.

In the bread aisle, she lingered over a pack of flour tortillas. They were large and golden and perfectly uniform. The packaging showed a grinning man in a sombrero. Ana thought of the paper parcels stacked in the *tortilleria* at Colony Felicidad, of Susanna's hands, sticky with corn-flour dough, and the sparkle of salt.

The lady at the checkout counter didn't look up as she scanned Ana's items, punched a code into her machine and turned the display reader so that Ana could read the amount. Ana had already inhaled to say "hello," feeling slightly giddy at the thought of speaking to someone, exchanging a few words, just so that she could remember how. When she saw that this wasn't going to happen, she swallowed instead, kicking herself for being so naive. People didn't talk here, not to strangers. Statistically, that made sense: there were more people, so more strangers. In Colony Felicidad, there were no strangers: always a "hello" at the very least, and more likely questions about yourself, your family, any time you saw someone for the first time in more than a few days. Nor would she be greeted simply by name but by a host of pet names, familiar names, secret names. Baby Bird, Miloh's girl, Sweet Ani. The lady at the checkout counter certainly didn't know any of those.

Then, a startling thought. *If no one knows who I am here, do I even exist?*

Ana returned home with forty-two cents in change, which she left on the kitchen counter for her father with the receipt.

—⁂—

Unwrapping the broccoli from its plastic, Ana started at the sensation of something small and black scurrying from between the stalks onto her hand and around her wrist before dropping into the sink. It lay there, curled in a puddle of dishwater, for several seconds before unfurling one leg—two, six . . . *eight* legs—and bracing itself against the foreign surface. It was brown, actually, not black, with a fat, hairy body and two sharp pincers at its front that might have been horns, or a claw.

Disgusting, thought Ana—and then she shivered at the recollection of its legs glancing her skin.

"Product of Brazil" said the sticker on the plastic wrap, which also had a barcode and the supermarket's logo on it. Brazil was a huge country that bordered Bolivia to the east; many of the trains from Santa Cruz were either coming from or going there.

Harnessing her revulsion, Ana peered more closely at the spider. She wondered if it was poisonous. She was tempted to run the water and wash it down the drain, but suddenly she felt sorry for it. Perhaps because it seemed so solid—more like an animal than an insect—and because it almost certainly hadn't known, when it clambered onto that particular head of broccoli one morning only days ago, that it would find itself shrink-wrapped and loaded onto a truck, then a plane, then another truck, before being piled onto a fridge shelf and left there until some girl came along and dropped it into her shopping basket.

She took a glass from the cupboard and looked around the kitchen for a piece of paper large enough to slide in under the glass. She would trap it gently and release it outside. She spotted the Phuket Paradise takeout menu on the counter and grabbed it. It had fallen through the letterbox three days ago, and neither Ana nor her father had known what to make of it. Now, at last, it had a purpose. Armed with the tools of capture, she turned back to the sink—

Nothing.

She stepped back from the counter, scanning the linoleum tiles, but it was impossible to make out a brown body against the swirl of mustard-colored flowers. She considered the countertops and even dared to push aside the mug tree in case it had sought refuge behind it, to no avail. The sink was deep and damp-splattered. Surely it couldn't have climbed out so quickly? Had it gone down the drain of its own accord, seeking safety in the dark? Ana took the flashlight from the cleaning cupboard and shone it down the plughole, but still couldn't see anything.

Even if she shut the kitchen door, the spider was small enough to crawl under it. Ana imagined herself lying in bed that night, waiting to hear the whisper of movement across her pillow, a tiny, hairy leg tickling her ear—

Ana, stop being stupid. It's gone down the drain. It's committed spider-suicide. Why would it want to go anywhere near your ear?

She rinsed the broccoli and placed it in a colander, which she put in the fridge. Then she re-opened the fridge, tore off one bushy broccoli stem and left it on a piece of paper towel on the counter by the sink. She did not know if it was a lure or a friendly gesture to a fellow-in-exile, and mainly she hoped that it would remain untouched.

"Good luck, amigo," she said. "Just stay out of my room."

The first time Suvi appeared at the front door, she was carrying a skateboard: black with yellow wheels and some kind of graffiti on the bottom. She spun it on one end as she tilted her head to the side and, squinting up at Papa, said, "Would your daughter like to come out?"

She was chewing bubble gum and rested one hand on her hip. Her wrist was stacked with fluorescent woven bracelets. The yellow wheels rattled.

Ana had watched through the banister railings on the landing. Papa had glanced up in time to see her flinch and disappear into the bedroom.

"She's not in," he said. "Perhaps another day? I'll tell her you came."

Two days later Suvi returned, this time without her skateboard. Her sneakers were squashed and dirty and covered in peace signs scribbled in black pen. She was eating a Fruit Roll-Up.

"We're going down to the ravine," she said to Papa. "This is Jonty and Ben; they live three doors down from you."

Behind her, a tall boy hovered in the middle of the street, chucking a tennis ball at some tree branches. A younger boy sat on the sidewalk, watching him.

Papa must have heard the whisper of the kitchen door shutting, must have sensed Ana leaning against it, holding her breath.

"I'm sorry," he said. "She's a little under the weather today."

That evening, he said to her, "She may not come again. If she does, you should go for a bit. She lives across the street. I've seen her parents. An only child, like you. Maybe you'll be friends."

The third time, Ana had no choice: she was sitting on the front step when Suvi came rattling up the sidewalk.

"Hey," she said. "Are you feeling better?"

She didn't wait for Ana to reply, but flipped her skateboard and ambled up the walkway.

"I'm Suvi," she said. "Jonty's got his bike down at my place." She held up a five dollar bill. "We can get Cokes from the store . . . if you want?"

Ana nodded.

"What's your name?"

"Ana."

"Have you got a board? Or a bike?"

"No."

"That's OK—I'll go slow."

—#—

Jonty and Ben only stayed for a little while, lounging over the handlebars of their bikes with closed faces.

"We're not really friends," said Suvi after they'd gone. "I just hang out with them in the summer. To be honest, I doubt they'd have come to your door if it hadn't been for me bugging them. They think girls are lame."

Ana was secretly relieved that they'd left. The taller one had stared at her as if she was something disappointing in a zoo, and she'd heard the younger one snort behind his hand, "Cool braids, Princess Leia." She didn't know what this meant, but she knew it couldn't be good.

"So, where'd you come from?" Suvi cocked her chin at Ana's sweatshirt. "I don't know that camp."

Ana glanced at her front, at the upside-down letters of Camp Kawinpasset. "Bolivia," she said. "South America."

It felt strange to be speaking in English, and she was suddenly grateful for the informal lessons she'd had from Aunt Justina, who had worked hard over the years to remember the language of her Albertan childhood.

"Whoa, cool. So you're Bolivian? But you're so pale!"

"My family's from Russia . . ." She motioned with one hand, searching for the word. "Before. A long time ago. They lived in Canada for a while, and then they went to Bolivia." Ana listened to herself, approving of the perfect circle her narrative seemed to be forming. "But now we're back in Canada." As if it all made sense.

"I get it. So, you're going to go to Walpole in the fall?"

"Excuse me?"

"For high school. It's either there or, uh, Upper Beaches?"

"I don't know." Ana paused. In Bolivia, she would have finished her schooling by now. "I don't think my father's decided yet."

"Well, you should totally try to come to Walpole. It's closer and it has a rock climbing wall. I've been going to the middle school there, so I kind of know my way around. We'd probably be going into grade nine together. Are you fourteen?" Ana nodded. "Me too. It was my birthday last month. That would be cool."

—⁎—

"No school," her father said.

He hadn't even looked up from the plank of wood that he was marking with a pencil.

"But I have to go. Suvi says it's the law." Ana watched her father straighten, using the pencil to scratch behind his ear. That word, *law*, had caught his attention.

"Suvi is the girl who came here?"

"Yes. She's nice."

"And she knows about the law? This thirteen-year-old girl?"

"Fourteen. She said the police had to escort some boy to school last year. He was living with another family. A foster family, I think she said . . ."

At last, her father looked at her.

"Leave it with me," he said. "I'll find out."

"Walpole," said Ana. "If I have to go, please can we make it Walpole?"

"I'll do as I said," came the reply. Then he nodded at the kitchen, her responsibility. "When I've finished here, we'll have dinner."

—⁎—

They called it her mother's pearl necklace, although the pearls weren't real. Ana didn't know where it had come from. Nobody she knew wore jewelry; in their community it would be considered a vanity. Her father tolerated its presence in the house only as long as it stayed in the box in the cupboard of the dry sink. Over the years the cord had worn thin, and the necklace had to be restrung. Ana's mother had taken it to a Bolivian man in the village who sold watch batteries and tightened earring clasps. She only went to him a few times, but on each visit he must have secretly taken a few pearls off and replaced them with plastic ones. You could tell a plastic pearl because it dented when you bit it. Now, all but three of the pearls on the necklace were marked with punctures where Ana had tested them.

"I don't know why you keep it," said her father. "It's worthless."

"It was hers."

"It wasn't. The real pearls were hers. Your mother was always too trusting."

Colony Felicidad

Gerhard Buhler had never liked Papa. In all our years in Colony Felicidad he never said as much, and neither did Papa, but somehow I always knew it. Perhaps the ripples from my mother's disappearance reached further than people were willing to admit. The light from a star continues to travel for many thousands of years after the star has died.

Or perhaps it had nothing to do with my mother. I just assume that it did because I only ever knew about one thing that linked them: when I was four she saved Gerhard Buhler's youngest boy, Isaac, from drowning.

You'd think this would be a good thing, the sort of thing that would make Gerhard Buhler forever grateful to her. We were on a day trip to the lake off Route Four—my mother and me, Maria and Susanna and Isaac, and a couple of other women with their children, plus Papa who drove us and Frank Reimer—because it was so hot.

The lake was the closest thing we had to the seaside because the Pacific Ocean is miles away, beyond Bolivia's borders and even past Chile and Peru. Instead we drove a couple of buggies down the drive and onto the main road and then onto another road that ran parallel to Route Four for about half an hour, and then down a track that led onto a secret slice of waterfront that hardly anyone ever sees. It's a freshwater lake, but the beach is a little sandy, so we could almost pretend it was the seaside. The beach is a thin sliver between the shining water and the trees, and the sand is gray, mostly damp.

The boys went swimming in their breeches. The women laid out blankets and stayed on shore, while my father and Frank Reimer took off their shoes and socks to walk in the shallows. Maria, who was almost fourteen then, tucked her skirts into her belt so that she could wade in up to her knees. Susanna and I and the other little girls went in in our slips. The water was cold and black and wicked against our skin.

After a while I must have left the water, as I remember sitting next to my mother, feeling the sun on my bare legs and the reassuring tug of her hands as she combed and re-braided my hair. That was a treat—usually we washed and braided only once a week—and I remember savoring the delicious indulgence of it.

I don't remember what happened in between that moment and the moment we were all standing at the other end of the beach, far from where we had set up our camp, right where there were some rocks bouldering the trees. My mother was in the water, and my father was running into the water after her to take Isaac Buhler in his arms, to pass Isaac to Frank, and then to help my mother out of the water, her skirts trapping between her legs, her face pale and gasping.

I don't know how she knew that Isaac Buhler was in trouble, because the rest of us would have thought you'd have to hear screams first: "Help me! I'm drowning!" Perhaps it was something she'd learned on her childhood farm in Alberta; perhaps there had been stories of little boys who drowned in watering holes there. Until then I'm not sure that anyone was aware my mother even knew how to swim, but I suppose she must have been pretty good to reach Isaac, who had drifted beyond the rocks and become caught in some old fishing nets. Either that, or she was just really brave.

I don't remember the rest of that day, although I do remember for a long time afterward the littlest kids saying, "Isaac Buhler is drowning" as though it was still happening, even though Isaac Buhler was alive and well and usually to be found burying ants in their anthills or stealing cream cookies from the kitchen. "Isaac Buhler is drowning" became something of a song after that, the kind of thing you sang rather than said. It didn't mean anything.

So why Gerhard Buhler had it in for Papa, I don't know. Maybe I'm getting things confused. Sometimes that happens when you're trying really hard to remember. The harder you try, the more confusing it all becomes.

Toronto

"SO, WHEN'S THE REST of your stuff arriving?"

They were standing in the middle of Ana's room, and Ana was wishing that she'd had time to put away the clothes her father had bought her. As it was, they were spread across the bed like outlines at a crime scene.

"This is it." Ana swallowed. "We left most of our things in Bolivia."

"Do you have a TV?"

Ana shook her head.

"That doesn't matter. You can watch most things online now, anyway." Suvi waited for Ana to respond. "Do you have a computer?"

Ana breathed deeply. "I think my father wants to get a new one. Ours is . . . broken." Anticipating more questions, she said, "We're getting a new car too."

"Cars are a hassle in the city, anyway," said Suvi. She pointed at the bed. "Interesting clothes," she said.

Not as interesting as my old ones, thought Ana.

"You having a garage sale or something?"

"I'm . . . sorting them. For charity."

"That's cool. Hey, so what did you say your parents do?"

"My dad's a carpenter. My mother . . ." Ana spotted the pearl necklace coiled in a dish on the windowsill. In Colony Felicidad, no one had ever commented on her mother's absence. "She died a long time ago."

"Oh, jeez. I'm sorry."

"It's fine." Ana forced cheeriness. "So, uh, can I see your house?"

Colony Felicidad

I tend to notice people's feet first, perhaps because I spend a lot of time looking down. Faces, especially new ones, can be kind of intimidating. Even with Aunt Justina, I preferred it when we talked sitting side by side. Using English felt like a kind of rebellion in a place where people only spoke German or perhaps a bit of Spanish, and it was something neither of us wanted to acknowledge. It was easier to practice conversation while looking at the long grass winding between our toes.

After my mother disappeared, I noticed how my father's feet changed. His shoes got dusty and the laces rarely got replaced. He went from stepping sure-footedly, almost restlessly, around the house to just kind of shuffling. I was too scared to look at his face for the longest time because of what I might see. And when he talked to me, I started to notice he felt the same way, because more often than not he'd talk to my feet instead, or else to a point just past my shoulder.

There were lots of interesting feet to watch at the airport in Santa Cruz. Callused heels in flip-flops; painted nails on tanned toes in wedge heels; enormous cushioned sneakers; black alligator skin sharpening to a business-like point; jelly sandals; and shoes with a little light in the heel that flashed when they moved.

I wondered where Papa had found the money to buy our tickets. I'd seen him put one of the boxes from the dry sink in his bag as we left. It held a gold watch that I'd assumed was once my grandfather's, and a few rolled-up notes of some foreign currency that were of no use to us in Bolivia. The box had once held my mother's pearl necklace too, only I'd taken that for my own years before.

Now that I think about it, I can't remember much about my mother's feet at all.

Toronto

"THIS IS JULIE, and that's Steve." Suvi reached across the kitchen island to dip a carrot stick in a bowl of something green and white. "Help yourself."

Suvi's mother looked like a grown-up version of Suvi, with the same square bob and blunt bangs and wobbly grin. Her skin was tanned, and she wore silvery purple eyeliner. She was dressed in a tank top, cut-offs and bare feet—her toes were painted bright coral pink, and there was a silver toe ring on her baby toe—and when Suvi introduced them she squeezed a hand around Steve's soft waist and smiled liked a schoolgirl.

"Hey, Ana. Nice to meet you. You're welcome to stay for dinner, if you like. We're doing tacos."

"Thanks. I may have to ask my father first."

"No problemo."

Steve was pouring a couple of beers into tall glasses. "Suvi says you moved here from Bolivia," he said. "Yikes."

"It's a long way away."

"You were born there?" Ana nodded. "I was born in Australia. Don't remember much about it now; we moved here when I was five. But I can still do a mean Aussie accent."

"No, you can't!" laughed Julie, rolling her eyes. "Don't encourage him, Ana."

"Come on," said Suvi, yanking at Ana's arm. "Let's leave the love-birds to their beer."

They went upstairs to Suvi's room, where the walls were covered in band posters and ticket stubs and pages of highlighted Blue Jays rankings from Sportsnet and tropical lights.

"Your parents are really nice," said Ana.

"Steve's my stepdad, actually. He's been here for a couple of years now. He's got a daughter too, Phoebe, but she's at university." Suvi squatted at a basket next to her bed that was stacked with magazines. "I've got the new *Seventeen*, if you want to look at it. I know it's kind of cheesy, but the sex advice is hilarious."

But Ana was looking at a pencil drawing taped to the back of the bedroom door: a girl who was definitely Suvi.

"Did you draw this?"

"No, my friend Mischa did it. He and his folks are up north right now—you'll meet him when they get back. So, what kind of music do you like?" She squinted at Ana. "I'm guessing you're not into boy bands."

Ana shrugged, waited. "I'm into indie." Suvi reached for a pile of vinyl records dominoed under the bed. "The Yeah Yeah Yeahs especially. I cut my hair like Karen O last spring. Who else . . . the Arctic Monkeys are pretty good. And Mogwai."

"I don't know them."

"Probably because they're Scottish." She pushed the vinyl aside. "So, what do you like to do for fun?" Ana shrugged again. "Like, Mischa, he draws. And he sings in this junior opera thing."

"What about you?"

"I like sports, I guess. Basketball in the fall, volleyball in the winter, baseball or soccer in the spring. Those are my school teams, anyway. In the summer I just loaf around and ride my bike and read trashy books and eat sour keys and check out the lifeguards at the pool."

"I like swimming." The words were out before Ana had weighed their full implication.

"Cool! We could go tomorrow, if you want? You look like a swimmer. Tall, I mean. Strong shoulders."

"I don't have a . . ." She gestured at herself. "It . . . it got left behind."

"You can borrow one of my swimsuits. Or, if that weirds you out, you can get one there—they usually have a few for sale by the cash."

"I'll have to ask my father."

"They're not expensive. Of course, they're not super sexy, either."

"That's OK."

"It's a date, then. Awesome!"

Awesome.

Across the street from the grocery store was a row of houses in varying stages of abandonment. Pointy-roofed Victorians with iron railings fencing off the entrances to dingy basement apartments. Some windows were hung with yellowing curtains, one or two had NO PLANES stickers, one was blocked with a sheet emblazoned with a marijuana leaf, and a few were boarded up completely. One of the houses had a gray metal door with a security buzzer and a discreet sign down by the bike racks that said EAST END WOMEN'S CENTER.

Ana never usually found herself on that side of the street since their house was on the same side as the grocery store. That day, though, leaving Suvi's, she remembered that she had promised her father that she would buy some rice for their dinner. So Ana headed toward the store on the west side. Waiting for the light to change, she noticed the sign.

Laminated blinds clattered in the window, disturbed by someone brushing against them on the other side of the glass. Ana caught a glimpse of a bookshelf crammed with leaflets, the fronds of a potted plant. She wondered what went on behind the metal door.

As if someone had been reading her thoughts, the door opened and two women came out. They were young, smiling. One had blond hair tied up in a turban; the other dark hair and long feather earrings that brushed her shoulders. As she waited for the turbaned woman to unchain her bike, the dark-haired woman took a pack of cigarettes from her bag and pulled a lighter from her back pocket.

"Excuse me," said Ana. Both women looked up at her, and she froze.

"Hey," said the turbaned woman. "What's up?"

"Can you tell me . . ." Ana looked up at the heavy metal door. *What? What was she trying to ask them?* It was a feeling, nothing more. An instinct.

"Did you want to go in?" said the woman with the feather earrings. "I can buzz you in."

"I'm just looking for someone."

Now it was their turn to freeze. Feather woman eyed Ana with new suspicion.

"There's confidentiality," she said. "You can't just walk in looking for someone."

"It's meant to be a safe place," said the turbaned woman, more gently. "For people in trouble. Are you in trouble?"

"No," said Ana quickly. *This could all go wrong. It could chase her further away—*

Turban woman nodded, exchanged a look with feather woman.

"We'll buzz you in," she said. "You can check in with reception. Youth hours are Tuesdays and Thursdays from four to nine, so if you hang around for half an hour you could go check out the games room upstairs. They have a coffee machine."

"Helena," Ana repeated. "But some people call her Lena. Rempel. Or maybe Doerksen—that's her married name."

"I'm sorry," said the woman behind the desk, which was cluttered with open binders, post-it notes and a stack of unopened mail. Her screensaver twisted with a parabola of constantly changing colors. Thank-you cards and pictures of teddies hugging stuffed hearts had been stuck to the wall behind the computer. "There's no one working here by any of those names. And I can't give out client information."

"Of course." Ana glanced up the narrow staircase. "Can I wait here for a bit?"

"Make yourself comfortable. There are magazines on the table."

The chairs were well-worn, the pink carpet faded by the sun but carefully vacuumed. Hanging ferns and wind chimes made the room feel homey.

Ana scanned the pamphlets in the window. *You Had Plans—A Baby Wasn't One of Them. Free HIV Testing. Women's Hotline, Free and Confidential. Domestic Abuse: The Facts.*

Behind her was a notice board. Ana twisted around to read some of the printouts and posters affixed there.

Stitch and Bitch, Wednesdays at 7 pm—All knitters welcome! Tea provided.

Anishinaabe language classes—free if you bring a friend.

Pride Week sign-up!!

Movie nights, Saturday in the games room. Sign up for your weekly date with George, Brad or Ryan!

Yoga classes—pay what you can. Space limited, so sign up now!

Baby and toddler play mornings at Cedar Ridge—parenting and family planning advice.

Ana turned around. On the table next to the magazines were a pot of pens and a stack of client registration forms.

She picked up one and turned it over to the blank side.

—⁂—

"Can I leave this here?" Ana passed the piece of paper over the reception counter. On it she had written *Helena (Lena) Rempel/Doerksen* and the address of the house where she and Papa were staying. "In case she comes in?"

"This is your address?" Ana nodded. "Phone number?"

"I don't have one."

The woman grunted.

"OK," she said. "I'll tell Cathy when she gets here—she works reception in the evenings."

"Thank you."

"Come back any time. Youth hours are on Tuesday and Thursday afternoons. I guess no one turned up today because it's so nice out. It's busier during the school year."

"Can you imagine having to do that?" Suvi reached into the canvas bag, fumbling between the rolled-up towels for the sunscreen. She tipped her head toward the pool to where an older girl was cutting a slow line through the water. The girl was clothed from wrist to ankle in a black robe, and a black scarf made a perfect circle of her face as she held her chin stiffly above the surface.

Ana tried not to stare. Suvi had caught her out a few times already: studying the features of the Korean woman in the corner store, the African bus driver waiting at the station for his shift to start. In the colony, everyone had looked the same, excepting the Bolivian workers. But here, every other face was a puzzle to Ana, layered with mystery—closed doors secreting other lives, other homes, far away.

"Is it because of her religion?" Ana asked.

"I guess." Suvi squirted a dollop of lotion onto her hand. "You should really use some of this—you look like you burn easily."

"Thanks." Ana gingerly smoothed the cream over her face, hands and feet. She had yet to take off her jeans and top, which rustled against the smoothness of Suvi's swimsuit.

Suvi pulled her T-shirt over her head and unzipped her shorts. Instinctively, Ana looked away, pretending to fumble with her own top.

"It must be really hard work, swimming like that," Suvi said. "That gown thing looks heavy. I bet it's itchy too."

"Maybe it's special. For going in the water."

"Maybe." Suvi snapped her shoulder strap flat. "So, are you coming?"

"You go. I'll be a second."

Ana watched Suvi go, her body long and lean and tanned and boyish from behind. She climbed up to the top of the highest diving board, where she pulled a double thumbs-up at Ana before launching over the water, gripping her knees in a cannonball. The splash sent waves lurching over the edges. The robed girl stopped mid-stroke, flinching at the water in her eyes, before sedately carrying on.

"Holy crap, it's cold," gasped Suvi, who had appeared, dripping, beside Ana once more. "I mean, it's nice, but it's cold. Are you a jumper or an edger?"

"What?"

"Do you jump in, or do you edge in?"

"Oh. I think I'm an edger."

"Well, get edging, then!"

There was no getting around it. The sunlight glaring off the deck was making Ana thirsty, and her skin was prickling under the layers of clothing. *No one cares*, she told herself. *Papa would never come here. It's only you who knows.*

She peeled off her jeans so that they pooled in a heap around her ankles and then, still sitting on the bench, made a slow exit from her top. That wasn't so bad. Her skin was ghostly white, but she wasn't the only pale one there. Standing up, though, was another matter.

"Where are the steps?"

"On that side. Can you be any slower?"

"OK, OK."

They walked together, Ana's confidence growing next to Suvi. When she stepped into the water, it was as though a memory shocked itself into her foot. Up to her knees, and the muscles in her legs began to relax. In up to her waist. She sat, playing at the surface with her palms. *Isaac Buhler is drowning.* Only that wasn't today. Today was just the sun on white concrete, droplets collecting on the tiny golden hairs on Suvi's arms, sunscreen splatted on a polished bench. She entered the water headfirst, cutting straight past the swirling black robes as they trailed after the girl in the headscarf.

On the walk home from the pool, Ana continued toweling her hair, the rats' tails straggling wetly down her back, wondering what she'd say to her father if he came home early.

Suvi popped another sour key in her mouth. "So, when are you getting your new car?"

"In a few weeks. It depends how long we stay here."

Suvi stopped. "You mean you're not staying for good?"

"It depends on . . . stuff. My parents—"

"I thought you said your mother was dead?" Suvi remained where she was. Ana looked at her, and noticed for the first time that one of Suvi's eyes was a slightly different shade of green from the other.

"She's been gone for a long time," Ana said. "Since I was five. It's easier to think of it that way." She reached for the bag of sour keys, hoping to distract her friend's attention. But Suvi pulled the bag back.

"How can it be easier to think of her as dead?" she said.

"No one talked about her where we used to live," said Ana. "My father and I don't, either."

"But don't you want to know where she is?"

"That's why we came here. To look for her."

"Maybe she went back to her family—that's what I'd do. Why don't you just ask them?"

"They don't live in the city. But my father already spoke with some cousins whose farm is nearby. She's here. He's sure of it."

"God . . ." Suvi offered her the bag again. "That's crazy. So, do the police know?"

"No. We're doing it ourselves." Ana reached into the bag, then stopped. "You can't tell anyone. Promise?"

"I swear. But how will you find her?"

"My father's asking friends of his. I want to look too, but it's kind of impossible."

Suvi looped a sour key onto her pinkie and bit, tugging the jelly with her teeth. "Have you tried going online?" she asked.

Colony Felicidad

Of course I thought it was all my fault. And so from that day on I spent every waking moment trying to be a good girl, trying to atone for what I thought was my crime. In case Papa decided to leave me too.

My only secret was reading in English. Justina loaned me books that she and my mother had brought with them when they came here from Alberta. Paperback fiction, mostly. School stories. I could sense that the language was old-fashioned, but I didn't care. It felt delicious, practicing the words under my breath as I lay in bed at night. I wasn't trying to be bad, but I certainly never wished for anyone to find out.

No one in Colony Felicidad had ever told us that teenagers were supposed to be rebellious. Some of the boys would smoke on a Thursday night, when the teenagers got to go unsupervised. Thursday nights and Sunday afternoons were reserved for that sort of thing: drinking alcohol and secret meetings with girls. The adults mostly turned a blind eye. "It needs to come out," they'd say. We weren't baptized into the church yet, so there weren't the same expectations of us. But mostly we wanted to be seen as adults. When you were an adult, everything was better.

This is what we believed, anyway.

There are three things I know about my mother. The first two come courtesy of my Aunt Justina.

First, she told me that my mother was crazy for Berliner dough-nuts. Berliners weren't something that Old Colony folk in Bolivia tended to make, so I don't know where she and Justina discovered them, but it must have been back in Canada when they were girls. In Canada they were filled with jelly, but in Bolivia they filled them with yellow cream and dusted the tops with sugar. Justina told a story about how she and my mother had a long-standing argument about the best way to make them—by injecting the filling into the doughnut with a pipe, or by sandwiching it between two halves and frying them until they stuck together—and how they had planned to let my father decide with a blind taste-test. That was before my mother ran away. The taste-test never happened.

Second, Justina told me that when they were really little—this was still back in Canada—she and my mother and their brother used to sneak up to one of the farmhouses they passed on the walk back from school and peer through the window of the room with the television set. In this way they watched reruns of *The Mickey Mouse Club* and *The Lawrence Welk Show* and other old-time programs that the old couple who lived there would watch. In the summer the window might be open, and then they could actually hear the soundtrack, whereas in winter the window was always shut and it was just the moving pictures. My mother's favorite thing was watching the four Lennon Sisters sing "Hi to You!" and "Tonight You Belong to Me."

"Hey there, hi there, ho there, try our hos-pi-tal-i-ty!" sang Justina. That was as much as she could remember.

The last thing I know is what she wrote in the note she left in my treasure box before she ran away. I still have it and not even Papa knows.

Be kind. Think first. Forgive me.
"So long could I stand by, a looker on."
Love, Mama

Toronto

THE QUOTATION WAS FROM Shakespeare. Ana found it online a few days after Suvi showed her how to do an Internet search at the local library.

It was Ana's first visit to a library. Anyone could go in and use the computers, read the magazines, borrow the books—

"Not just books," said Suvi. "DVDs too. You know, movies. And video games. They're mostly lame and educational."

"How much does it cost?"

"It's free. It's run by the city. You just bring in your address—"

"But who owns it?"

"The city. Everyone."

"But . . ." Ana pulled a book off the shelf. "I could take it and not bring it back."

"You'd be a dick. And you'd get a fine."

Ana looked at the book in her hands. It was titled *A Taste of Italy*. On the cover was a burly older man with a fat mustache holding a fish. Ana slid it back onto the shelf.

At first Suvi had seemed excited to show Ana how to browse the Internet—"it's like a telephone book and a library and tons of takeout menus and a hang-out zone and a gallery and TV all in one!"—but soon she'd grown bored with the rate at which Ana wanted to stop and linger over every new page.

Even now, it took Ana a painfully long time to find the right letters on the keyboard, and the cursor kept swinging out of view as she maneuvered the mouse off the edge of the mouse pad, but finally, ignoring the looks of a couple of boys watching a music video at the computer opposite hers, she pressed "Enter." And there was her answer.

It was a line from *The Winter's Tale*, spoken by a character called

Perdita. Ana had first Googled the name in images, hoping that a photograph of her mother would miraculously appear. Instead, she had been confronted with thousands of pictures of a cartoon dog from something called *101 Dalmatians*, and a smattering of shots of airbrushed models and women in old-fashioned dresses. She had hovered over an image of a painting from the nineteenth century, of a porcelain-skinned woman with long red hair and laurels around her head and shoulders, and then she had turned to the online encyclopedia that Suvi told her contained information on almost any subject she could think of.

Perdita (Latin: "the lost girl") was the daughter of Leontes, King of Sicilia, and his wife Hermione. She was born in a prison where her father had sent her mother because he wrongly believed she had been unfaithful to him. He commanded one of his men to leave the infant on the seacoast to perish, but the servant took pity on the child and let her live, to be raised by a lowly shepherd. Sixteen years later, and now a beautiful young woman, Perdita remained unaware of her royal heritage. Prince Florizel fell in love with her, but because his father disapproved of the match they fled together to Sicilia, where her true identity was revealed and Perdita was reunited with her parents.

"Why didn't you stop her?" Papa had asked Ana once, in the heat of an argument the source of which Ana could no longer remember. "She had been sleeping in your bed. Any other child would have woken up or made a sound. We could have stopped her. *You* could have stopped her."

Ana stared at the computer screen. The results of a previous search were still open in another tab. "Kalahari ecosystem." Apparently, tribesmen in the Kalahari used something called the persistence method to hunt kudu. It meant they ran after their prey, but at a steady pace rather than a sprint, so that in effect they could run for days until the kudu had to give up.

Perhaps Ana could outrun her mother.

The next time Ana visited the Women's Center, a different lady was sitting at the reception counter. She beamed at Ana, showing teeth dotted with multi-colored braces.

"I left a note for someone," Ana said. "In case she came in. Helena Rempel? Or Doerksen. She might be called Lena."

The receptionist squinted at Ana, then something in her head seemed to click.

"Oh, right!" she said. "You're the girl . . ."

Ana felt her stomach leap.

The receptionist fiddled about after something in a drawer. She pulled out the paper with Ana's address written on it.

"This is you?" she said, pointing. Her nails sparkled with purple glitter polish.

"Yes," whispered Ana, her mouth suddenly dry.

The receptionist nodded.

"Becca told me," she said. "I'm afraid no one's come in by that name. I'll totally pass this on if she does, though."

She smiled cheerily at Ana as though she'd just said something wonderfully helpful. Ana swallowed.

"Oh," she said. "Thank you."

"No problem. Any time!"

—⚓—

"Hey," said Suvi, as Ana opened her front door. "Look who I brought."

On the step next to her stood a boy their age. He looked up through a curtain of dirty-blond hair, shoving his hands in his pockets and pulling them out again. He wore white tennis shoes with no socks and a braided cotton anklet.

"Hi," he said. "I'm Mischa."

"Hi," said Ana. "Ana."

"You guys want to get popsicles?"

After stopping at the corner store, they carried on to the baseball field. There was a huge expanse of flat, mown lawn, and a steep flight of concrete steps cutting through the ravine up to the main road. *This is what counts for nature here,* thought Ana. It wasn't as though the city lacked green space—there were parks and playgrounds and patches of forest with creaking wooden walkways; and parks crisscrossed with bike paths, studded with splash pads and water fountains and covered garbage bins; and empty lots with long grass and ticks and Lyme disease—but it was all managed. Someone had always cut the grass or weeded the concrete. There were no orchards, no fields so vast that you could run for hours with the dogs weaving ahead and behind you, where the corn grew tall enough to swallow you up—

"Mischa lives on the other side of the river," said Suvi. "He used to live next door to me, but then his grandma died and left his folks lots of money so they upgraded to a nicer 'hood.'"

"Your 'hood's not *not* nice."

"Yeah, but the houses in yours are huge. We'll go there next time, OK, Ana?"

"*Jo.*"

"Huh?"

"Yeah . . . yeah."

They climbed halfway up the bleachers and Suvi lay down with her legs hooked, upside-down, over the next step.

"Any adventures at your cottage this summer, Meesh?"

"Our septic tank blocked a few times. Grumpy got fed up with my lame-ass attempts at water-skiing after, like, twenty minutes."

"Other kids?"

"I met a guy who was staying in the place three houses down. From Ottawa. Grade ten."

"Ooh. Get his number?"

Ana watched Mischa's ears turn bright red as he bit off the end of his popsicle, dripping purple droplets onto the wooden bleacher. "Yeah."

"Sweet. Hey, Jerome is still lifeguarding at the pool. He wasn't there when I went with Ana, but I think he may just have been sick or something."

"Sick of you drooling over him."

"Shut up." Suvi poked her orange-stained tongue at him. "You have to make me sound cool in front of Ana. You can't come back and shatter my image, OK?"

Mischa grinned, rolling his eyes at Ana. "Whatever."

"Ana, I was telling him about how you used to live in Bolivia. Hey, so you speak Spanish? No offense or anything—is that what's going on with your accent?"

Ana licked the popsicle stick dry, shaking her head. "No, Low German," she said. She would have preferred just to listen to them talk instead, to make herself invisible.

"Is that what they speak there?"

"Just some people. Certain groups. My grandparents and mother were born in Canada, though. So they always spoke English, as well as German."

"Not, like, German-from-the-war kind of groups, though, right?" said Mischa. "My grandfather told me how loads of Nazis escaped to South America. War criminals and stuff."

"Jesus, Mischa—are you asking her if she's a Nazi?"

"A Nazi?" The word meant nothing to Ana. Which war were they even talking about?

"No, no!" This time, he blushed right down to his neck. "I didn't mean that."

"It's OK," said Ana. She decided to try again. "It's a Christian community."

"Like a cult?"

"I don't know . . ."

"What's it called, then?"

———#———

"Mennonites?" said Suvi, dropping her popsicle stick through a gap in the bleacher. "Like the Amish? Wagons and beards and headscarves and six wives and stuff?"

"The Amish don't get six wives," said Mischa.

"Neither do Mennonites," said Ana.

They wanted to know why, if her grandparents and her parents came from Canada, they had ended up in Bolivia. Ana explained that in the 1960s some of them started to get annoyed because the government wanted them to send their children to English-language schools and show them films about sex education.

"The first place my grandparents' community tried in Bolivia was in the middle of the desert," she said. "All they could see were scrub trees and thornbushes. My father's mother cried at the sight of all that empty space. They didn't even have clean drinking water. They stayed for a few days and most of them got dysentery and had to be taken back to the first camp they'd stopped at, near the border. There was a big fight with some of the elders, but eventually they all agreed to build the new community in the jungle instead. It was just as isolated as the desert, but things grew there."

They lived in a house with one wall dividing them from cows and chickens, and they set themselves to work clearing the rainforest and planting in unfamiliar soil. It was hotter than anything they'd ever experienced and the work was harder than usual because the land was so different from what they were used to farming, and the elders wouldn't bend the rules about not using modern equipment. In the end, some of the families returned to Canada—but Ana's paternal grandparents stayed on. Later, her mother's family moved there too.

"They kept their Canadian passports, though," she said. "Just in case."

"In case of what?" said Suvi.

Ana turned the popsicle stick over between her fingers, laid it flat. Picked it up again. "I don't know," she said at last.

The others seemed to accept this. Mischa said his parents were expecting him home for dinner, so they parted at the train tracks and Suvi waved good-bye to Ana outside her house. Only Ana heard in her answer a resonating question, which burrowed deep in her mind late into the evening.

Colony Felicidad

Susanna's mother used to tell us children never to talk to people outside the colony, in case we were kidnapped.

"The cities and towns are the Devil's playground," she would say.

"No one would want to kidnap Isaac," Susanna told me many times. "Or Maria. She talks too much."

"What about Eva?"

It was easy to imagine the Devil wanting Eva: plump, pink and golden, giggling Eva. Susanna angled her head, conceding this as a possibility.

"That's why we watch out for each other," she said. "That's why we're lucky to live here."

Toronto

ANA REMEMBERED THAT CONVERSATION with Susanna like it was a dream.

She couldn't ask Suvi what she thought. Suvi was nice, but Ana hardly knew her and Suvi wouldn't understand. The idea that cities and towns were places of sin wasn't something that Suvi would get. She'd probably want to tell Ana about all the perverted stuff that happened behind closed doors in the sunny suburbs.

Perhaps this was all part of it, though; perhaps Suvi herself was part of some larger plan to lure Ana away from everything she had been taught. As soon as she formed the thought, Ana rejected it as ridiculous.

That was the problem. If Ana started to question everything she had been taught in the colony, she might eventually have to ask why she and her parents had ever lived there in the first place. Doubting thoughts were the Devil's temptations.

Did she believe that, still?

If she didn't, had the Devil won?

---#---

"Are there other places like this?" Ana asked the receptionist. It was the older one again, the one called Becca. "Around the city, I mean."

"Um . . ." Becca seemed to weigh her words. "Yes. Lots. Do you have reason to believe she might be in this area?"

"I don't know." Ana felt her eyes start to burn. *Of course I don't. I don't even know if she's in Toronto . . .*

"Would you like me to give you some addresses? We have a sister branch in the Junction, and I've heard really good things about a new center on Kennedy—"

Ana shook her head. Her cheeks were beginning to ache with the effort of not crying in front of this woman.

"It's kind of hard for me to get around. There's probably no point."

Becca pursed her lips together.

"I'll send a few emails," she said. "Put her name out there and see if anyone comes back to me. I can't promise anything, though."

The purple ribbons had been there ever since they'd arrived. Tied around every streetlight, every tree, attached to front gates and bicycle racks for several blocks up and down their street, and all along both main roads to the north and south. At first Ana had wondered at their meaning, then she had grown used to them. Only when Suvi stopped one day to adjust one that had started to loosen and slump, bedraggled by summer storms, did Ana think to ask why they were there.

"For Faith Watson," came the reply. "The missing girl."

Ana felt something skim her shoulders, trailing ice down her spine. "Who?" she said.

"She used to live around here. Her parents and her brother still do. She's been missing since, like, forever." Suvi tugged the bow tight and flared the crinkled paper loops. "She's older than us, but still in high school. Sixteen or seventeen, I guess. Really pretty."

"What happened?"

Suvi tipped her head with an exasperated sigh. "If we knew, then she wouldn't be missing, would she?"

"There must be something."

"Loads of people phoned the police with tips when it happened. There was a kind of creepy security video of a guy in a van cruising around the neighborhood a few days before she went. I guess it didn't lead to anything, though—that was last spring."

They carried on, and eventually Suvi started saying how much she wanted to go to the new gelato place that had opened nearby, the one that did all those crazy flavors. "Bacon and blue cheese," she grimaced. "Artichoke and mustard. Beer, even . . ." But as she chatted on about the difference between ice cream and frozen custard, Ana found herself counting the purple ribbons that they passed, each one looking more forlorn than the last. What would Faith Watson think if she could see them, if she was here? Assuming she was even alive.

What must her family feel, seeing them now, listless and discolored? At what point did they stop being a sign of hope and become instead a painful reminder that Faith was still missing? Ana tried to imagine a purple ribbon tied around the *tipu* tree in Colony Felicidad. Or perhaps a red ribbon, because *tipu* trees bleed when they're cut—the resin oozes like ox's blood.

"I should go home," she said.

Suvi stopped and gave her a funny look. "Are you OK?"

Ana nodded. "I forgot I promised my father I'd make a nice dinner tonight."

"We're halfway to Buck's Scoop now."

"Some other time, I promise."

"OK, whatever. Hey, I'll still pick you up on the way to Meesh's place tomorrow?"

"Of course."

———#———

Tonight, she would bring Colony Felicidad here. For an evening, they could be home again.

Justina and Maria and Susanna had always helped her with the cooking. They had shared meals with her to serve to her father, and they passed on their recipes and kitchen secrets. Preparing meals was a social time, and Ana had been the child: observing, learning, listening.

Now, of course, things were different. Perhaps *because* things were different, Ana decided to make something she had not made before: her aunt's beef and cheese empanadas.

Hoping to conserve oil, Ana greased the pan as thinly as she dared. Bad idea. Within moments half of the beef had burnt on the bottom, which meant adding more potatoes to make up for the lost mince. Still, after half an hour the kitchen had filled with all the right aromas, and Ana poured the contents of the pan into a bowl to set while she got on with the pastry.

When her dough crumbled, she added water and kept kneading. More water. Before she had time to notice what was happening, she found her fingers poking through a sticky, stringy mess. By now there was no flour left, so nothing left to do but roll the dough into discs as best she could. She left the big ball of dough under a damp towel, just as her aunt always did. There was no lack of moisture, but going through the motions made Ana feel that she was doing something right. Steeling her resolve, she spooned a dollop of filling onto one disc. At least everything still smelled pretty much as it was supposed to.

The discs were too thin, though, and too sticky; without exception, each one tore as she stuffed it. In the end, Ana could only fill each pocket with the tiniest bit of beef filling in order for them to hold together, before twisting the edges to make a seal.

Six o'clock: half an hour before her father would be home. In her haste, Ana didn't wait for the oil to heat properly before dropping in the first empanada. It sank to the bottom and took several minutes to float to the surface. When she finally managed to fish it out of the pot it was an oily, soggy mess.

Nineteen to go, Ana told herself.

The plate she set before her father was a far cry from what she had imagined. Instead of crispy, golden empanadas, the best she had managed was a pile of pasty, slick lumps piled like a stack of tumors in an oily puddle.

"Empanadas," said her father, spearing one with his fork. Ana watched as he sliced it open, took a bite. He pulled his lip, rolled his head. "They're good," he said.

They were not good. There were too many potatoes, so the filling was starchy and bland. The pastry was slippery, the smell of oil overpowering. As she forced mouthful after mouthful, Ana felt the tears begin to build behind her eyes.

"They're awful," she said.

"They're not," he told her. "Look, we are eating them."

Only because it would be a waste not to, she thought. *Only because the one thing worse than eating them would be having to look at that pile of disgusting dough balls for a second longer.*

Later that night, Ana listened to the sound of her father tiptoeing downstairs . . . the rustle of bread being pulled from its bag . . . the fridge door opening . . . a knife slicing cheese on the linoleum counter.

Of course he's still hungry, she thought, as her own stomach clenched and gurgled. She felt a stab of annoyance and briefly considered going into the kitchen and catching him red-handed. *Dinner wasn't good enough?*

Dinner had been awful. Awful because she didn't have the first idea how to be a housewife here. How to be *anything* here.

It was a relief to cry, to allow the waves of hurt and humiliation and helplessness pour into her pillow until it was soaked. At the sound of the kitchen light being switched off, Ana held her breath, listening to her father climb the stairs and return to his room. After another moment, a door shut.

Crying seemed pointless in this darkness and silence; she was too alone even for self-pity. And so she stared into the gathering darkness, feeling herself harden with resolve. No more fancy cooking. No more attempts to make it better for him, either. Things were different now.

Tomorrow, they would start again.

There was music everywhere in the city: blasting from cars, thrumming through stores, jangling out of cell phones, the tinny remnants buzzing out of people's headphones. Always caught in snatches. And always, to Ana, the sound of it seemed intrusive, imposed. Not a part of the world. Not a part of her.

In Colony Felicidad, there had been singing in church, always unaccompanied. "The human voice is the purest instrument with which to sing God's praise," said Mr. Harms, her favorite minister. And Ana had loved the sound of the voices corded together like tall stalks reaching for the sun, the simple beauty of it, and the feeling that she could be a part of it too. Suvi talked about bands and singers as though it was all code for something—what was cool, what wasn't cool—but the voices in church didn't need translating.

"My Life Is a Pilgrimage." "How Great Is Your Almighty Goodness." "As the Deer Panteth." Those were Ana's favorites, the ones she would still catch herself humming unawares, the ones she would allow herself to sing when she was sure her friends wouldn't hear— as she cooked dinner, as she washed her hair. Perhaps Mr. Harms had been right about the human voice. It was something you could take wherever you went. No matter how far, it was always possible to sing yourself home.

—#—

Mischa sang too. "Old stuff," Suvi called it, because a lot of the songs were by dead composers or in dead languages. It seemed fitting, then, that Mischa's parents ran a home for old folks in a neighborhood full of tall, brick Victorian houses. Mischa and his parents lived on the top floor, and the old people lived on the second and third floors. Downstairs there was a kitchen and a dining room and a living room, which they called "the parlor," and a TV room with a pool table that the old men used to rest their canes against. The house smelled like Lysol and old flowers and backed onto a graveyard.

"Actually, it's called a necropolis," Mischa told her. "It means city of the dead."

Ana wondered what it was like for the old people to look out their bedroom windows and see the very place they would probably end

~ 44 ~

up in the relatively near future. She and Suvi and Mischa were sitting in Mischa's tree house, overlooking an undulating plain of neatly tended headstones and tree-lined footpaths. School would start in two days—something that neither seemed to excite or bother Suvi or Mischa. So Ana too had to play it cool, repressing the urge to ask a hundred questions about what she should expect.

"It's called a necropolis if there are actual tombs," Mischa was saying. "With bodies in them. Above ground." He brushed some brownie crumbs off his shirt and crawled over to the edge of the platform where a rope ladder hung. "Come and see."

They followed him past weeping angels and crosses and urns with shrouds draped over them until they reached a headstone made of what looked like red marble. It was divided into two halves, left and right. On the left, the name Henry Wilson Crombie, followed by the dates 1937–2010. On the right, Jane Erin Crombie—but no dates.

Was Jane Erin Crombie still alive? wondered Ana. What if she'd changed her mind? What if she no longer wanted to be buried next to Henry Wilson Crombie? In an instant, Ana's pity shifted from Jane—poor, haunted Jane—to Henry. Jilted, betrayed Henry, left waiting for all eternity.

"What if she remarried?" she said to Suvi.

"That would be kind of ironic."

"Ironic?"

"Irony. You know, like, different from what you hoped for. Like the guy who invented poison gas in the First World War dying in the gas chambers in the Second World War because he was Jewish. That's kind of ironic. Or Captain Hook being the bad guy and also Wendy's father—"

"Is that really in the story?" asked Mischa.

"Different from what you hoped for," repeated Suvi with a shrug. "But in a kind of bad way."

Colony Felicidad

When the police asked, we didn't tell them that Papa had been there the night it happened. Aunt Justina shot me a look that told me not to answer their questions, and while she didn't lie outright she left out a few details that could have made things different for us.

It was unusual for the police to come all the way out to Colony Felicidad. It was unusual for them to take any interest in us at all. Judging by reports we heard from some of the older boys after their trips into town, the police had more than enough to keep them busy in Santa Cruz. The latest story doing the rounds was about a gang that was orchestrating illegal adoptions of Bolivian kids and making a heap of money along the way. There was even a rumor that one baby had been smuggled out of its village inside a watermelon.

The police came back a few days later, when Papa was in. That time they asked to speak to him. I sat on the other side of the wall with Susanna's little sister Eva, making shadow puppets with my hands over a piece of paper so that she could trace the outline with her pencil. We did a bird, a donkey, a dog and a woman in a full skirt before the door opened and Papa asked me to go and find Gerhard so the police could speak to him.

The next day, he told me to pack my bag and said if anyone asked our surname was Rempel. That was my mother's maiden name. Later, I learned that Picasso had taken his mother's maiden name too, but for different reasons. Had I known this then, perhaps it would have seemed exciting and even a bit romantic, to say that from now on my name was Ana Rempel. But it was different then, and not in a good way.

Toronto

AT LAST ANA HAD GOT the hang of the washing machine. It was ancient and noisy, and jolted and shimmied and rumbled a good four feet across the concrete floor each time she ran it—it always had to be pushed back afterward, into the dark corner shared with the boiler in their basement—but their clothes came out smelling OK and usually the right color. There wasn't a dryer, and it was too dank and crowded in the basement to hang things there, so Ana had to wait for dry days to pin things on the washing line outside their back door. Perhaps it was the soap they used here, or the water, but everything always dried stiff and crusty; she had to shake and roll and tussle their clothes just to make them wearable. Towels dried like cardboard on good days, sandpaper on bad.

Once, when she'd gone to the washroom at Suvi's house, Ana found herself idly opening a slatted wooden door next to the bathtub. Inside were shelves and shelves of perfectly folded towels: bath towels, hand towels, face cloths, beach towels, a couple of spare bath mats. Ana had touched one gingerly to see if it was as soft as it looked. It was.

Justina used to help Ana with the washing at Colony Felicidad, and their towels had been like this. Blankets too had been plain, but soft. They felt of home. There was nothing of her own scratchy, rigid laundry drying on the line behind Mrs. Fratelli's house that felt of home.

Without thinking, Ana pulled one of the large beach towels from Suvi's airing cupboard and shook it out. It was blue, with a hot pink and green striped trim. The cupboard was warm; the towel smelled of lavender. Ana wrapped it around her shoulders and pulled the corners up to her nose. Cradled in its embrace, she crouched on the edge of the bath and began to cry.

---#---

"Everything OK?" said Julie, poking her head round the bedroom door as Ana emerged from the bathroom.

"Yes, fine. Thanks."

Julie dropped whatever it was she was busy folding onto the bed and stepped out onto the landing.

"I'm so glad you guys have become friends," she said. "It's nice for Suvi to have a girl to hang out with. There aren't any other girls your age on the street, and so many of the kids go away in the summer. I think you're a very good influence on her. Steadying, I mean."

Ana nodded.

"You'll let us know if there's ever anything you need, right? You and your dad too."

"I will. That's very kind of you."

Julie stretched out her arms and pulled Ana into a tight hug. At once Ana felt the tides begin to pull at her chest again; her eyes, just splashed with cold water a minute ago, began to burn. How long had it been? She was aware that she was clinging to Julie's shoulders—tight, tight, like a buoy bobbing far out to sea—but she didn't care. Just as long as Julie didn't see her cry.

At last, when she felt she could trust her voice not to waver, she pulled away.

"Suvi's good at lots of stuff, but hugs aren't her forte," smiled Julie. "They're on the house here whenever you fancy."

"Thanks," said Ana. "I'll remember."

---#---

The town of Moth didn't exist for thirty years, because in 1920 the people at *National Geographic* messed up and left it off the atlas. It had always been a small town, but over the course of those thirty years it got even smaller. The *National Geographic* thing shouldn't have made a difference—just because a place doesn't show up on a map can't mean that the people who live there just stop working and getting married and having kids—so maybe that was a coincidence.

People always pointed out that Moth isn't a very Spanish name, or even a Guaraní one. The town was founded in 1859 by a man called Tomas de Molli, who dreamed of starting a porcelain works on the border with Chile, using the sodium nitrate mined from the salt-peter fields to make beautiful ceramics to be sold all over the world. He thought he'd get all his friends and family from Europe to move there with him, but most of them found that living in the middle of a saltpeter field wasn't all that old Tomas had cracked it up to be, so a lot of them left. The town was supposed to be called Molli, but the first person to record it in the census or deed poll or mapping project or whatever it was made it look as though the first "L" was a "T," and the second "L" and the "I" joined up to look like an "H." So Moth was born.

Ana had never been to Moth, although it existed in her imagination more vividly than the house she had grown up in until the day Papa said they were leaving Colony Felicidad. In her mind, Moth was a village of sugar-cube houses set in the middle of a vast, flat, salty-white plain. There was a palm tree growing in front of each house, so that the families could sit outside and still be shaded from the harsh sun. There was a well in the town square—little kids threw marbles and kicked a soccer ball up against it—and a church with a bell tower. In her mind, it was always 1859 in Moth, and Tomas de Molli is often to be seen making his rounds, trailed by a little Guaraní boy whom he has adopted as his son. Tomas de Molli is a wiry, tightly coiled man with a black beard and hooded eyes. He wears a broad-brimmed straw hat and a white peasant's shirt tucked into trousers that spill over the top of dust-coated boots. The little boy who fol-lows him is called Popi; the dog that follows Popi is called Sue. Tomas and Popi and Sue go everywhere together.

The only reason Ana had heard of Moth was that it was used in the colony as a shorthand for getting in over your head, finding yourself in a sticky situation without means for escape. "He's gone to

Moth" is what people would say if they saw a cat stuck up in a tree, or if they were listening to one of the boys try to explain his way out of skipping school, weaving one lie out of another until he couldn't be sure where his story started or ended.

When Ana was eight, she had been surprised to spot a bus barreling down the main road with "MOTH" spelled out in flip-down letters on its destination window. A few years later, she heard it mentioned as a place where convicts sometimes gave themselves up to the police—not on purpose, but because it was the last town before the Chilean border, so it was where a lot of police chases ended up.

That information didn't agree with the picture Ana had built up of the sugar-cube houses and the church tower and Tomas de Molli making the rounds with Popi and Sue, so she tried to bury it. She didn't know then how impossible this would be.

Toronto

WALPOLE SECONDARY SCHOOL was one giant cinder block: ungainly, beige. Along the front and sides the concrete had been sculpted into modernist ribbing, leaving slits for windows. A long, flat-roofed extension on the east side was the middle school, where Suvi and Mischa had gone for the last two years: Suvi pointed it out before steering Ana towards the high school entrance at the front of the main building. The back wall was solid stucco, apart from a fire exit leading from the gym. There was a parking lot, and off of it a basketball court that was virtually identical to the parking lot, only without cars or yellow lines. There was a field of flattened yellow grass with football posts and a broken picnic table.

It should have looked nicer than this, set as it was on a tree-lined street, flanked by houses with baby-carrier bike attachments chained to the front gates, SUVs discreetly parked in the laneways behind. Houses like Jonty and Ben's.

"Jonty and Ben go to Upper Canada College," said Suvi, when Ana asked why they weren't walking to school together. "They get a ride there with their dad on his way to work." Then she added, as if to stop Ana from envying them their fancy private school, "They have to wear *uniforms*."

Ana would have killed for a uniform. Uniformity was what school in Colony Felicidad had been about. But then school in Colony Felicidad had also meant only twenty children in a one-room schoolhouse. Chickens clucking in the doorway. Wood-framed slates for practicing sums and handwriting. The Bible, hymnbooks and a few yellowing and dog-eared primers collecting dust on a window ledge. Afterward, *kringel* with Susanna and Eva and the Hamm sisters and their cousin under the *tipu* tree, which bloomed with yellow flowers at the start of the school year.

Standing in front of Walpole Secondary School, Ana thought of Popi, the little Guaraní boy she once imagined had been adopted by Tomas de Molli. She thought of him living alone in the bush—perhaps his parents had died of plague or in a blood feud—and spying a tall bearded man through the pampas grass one morning. Popi would never have seen skin so white or a beard so long. The man's hat would have looked silly, and yet Popi would covet it.

The kids flowing into Walpole Secondary School were white, black, Asian, South-Asian—different from each other but most of all different from Ana in the way they walked, the way they shouted, the roughhousing of the boys and the slouching sly looks of the girls. Ana was transfixed: fascinated and terrified. This school was a new country, and she was an interloper.

—⧸⧸—

"Remember your combination," said Suvi, testing the lock with a shake. "Write it in sequence on three different pages in your agenda in case you forget."

What Ana wanted to say was, *Why do we need to keep schoolbooks and lunch bags and gym socks and pictures torn from magazines locked up in a metal container?*

Instead, she said, "I don't have anything that valuable."

"Doesn't matter. Oh, and the school can check your locker at any time. Lots of kids think they have to ask permission, but they don't."

What are they looking for? Ana wondered. And, as if she'd read her mind, Suvi said, "Weed, man, weed. Some doofus gets caught every year."

"Hey, cutie. Talk to me!"

Both girls looked up as a locker slammed shut behind them. Across the corridor, a boy in a gray hoodie stood smirking at his phone. He slid it into his back pocket and hauled his bag over one shoulder before sloping off toward the fire exit.

Suvi rolled her eyes. "Justin Cook."

"Did he say something?"

"That was his ringtone. His girlfriend's voice. Karen brings him his lunch every day—in middle school it was always a six-inch sub from the Belly Buster across the street." Suvi picked up her bag. "Makes me barf. If it wasn't for Karen, he'd be cool. He has a band called, like, Diamond Fraction. Or Diamond Divided, or something." She nudged Ana with her elbow. "Irrelevant information, dude. He's not our type."

There were two classes before lunch. Suvi delivered Ana to English after showing her the shortcut to her math class. Surrounded by noisy strangers, Ana had never felt more alone. She was relieved when the teacher walked in and placed an overstuffed bag on the desk. She managed to regulate her breath and thumping heart while course outlines were handed up and down the rows, reading lists distributed, literacy test forms explained. The information sailed past her in a blur; she would have to get Suvi to explain it to her later.

The bell that rang to signal the end of the lesson made her jump noticeably enough that a couple of girls in the row next to her exchanged looks and sniggered. There was a surge of bodies at the doorway. The teacher escaped ahead of her students. There was no dismissal, no thank-yous, no orderly lining up.

In math, the desks were organized in groups. The teacher, when he arrived, wanted this changed. At first Ana thought he must be the caretaker, or perhaps the principal, because she assumed that the same woman who had them for English would teach them every-thing. Not so. The students were rowdy as they heaved the desks into rows, laughing and chattering. Ana was glad of the delay; she knew that math here was taught differently, that she would be far behind. There was comfort in physical work, shifting desks and chairs, col-laborating with the others without having to say a thing. She began to relax.

She was relaxed enough to pay attention to the lesson. It was another language to her. Once again, the teacher was gone before she could ask him how she was supposed to complete the homework. It was something else to ask Suvi, who was advanced at math.

The clock on the wall said 11:50 when the double bell rang for first lunch. Ana's stomach had been so tightly clenched all morning that she had forgotten to be hungry. Now, though, it was as if her body realized that she hadn't eaten since dinner last night. She scooped the plastic bag of corn muffins and cured sausage from her locker and waited.

"It's like some people got the memo that we're in high school now in giant capital letters," said Suvi, sliding her lunch tray onto the table and climbing over the bench. "Like: WE MUST BE DIFFERENT NOW. Have you noticed that, Meesh?"

Mischa grunted, continuing to shade a sketch of his milk carton in his notebook.

"Different how?" said Ana. She was surprised to hear herself almost shouting. The gym resounded with voices and lunchtime clatter, crowds of students flocking in like cattle at feed time. No orderly lines, no silent mealtime prayer. She poked at her food.

"Like Katie Greer. She grew like three inches over the summer and now she has boobs, but was that enough? Uh-uh. She has to start talking in this, like, deep growly voice that's supposed to sound sexy—"

"Says who?" said Mischa.

"Bex Kinnear, for one. Who, by the way, is all, 'I don't shave my legs, I only ever wax because if you shave the hair grows back thicker'—but she can't say it like a normal person, she has to ask everything? Like, say it as though it's a question? Even if it's not? What is even WITH that?" Suvi paused to consider the piece of sausage Ana had broken onto a corn muffin. "Dude, don't you want to buy lunch like everyone else?"

"It's expensive. This is fine."

Mischa smirked. "I hear Bex hooked up with Cory Shyman at camp," he said.

"What's so funny, Aleeshah-Meesha-Juanita-Keesha?" Three boys Ana recognized from her homeroom swept up behind them, one grabbing Mischa by the shoulders and affecting a friendly wrestle.

"Watch out—he might think you're feeling him up."

"Good summer, Meesh, my man?"

"Spend it with your fag hags, bro?" said the tallest one, helping himself to Mischa's plate of French fries.

"Piss off, Fraser," muttered Mischa. Ana noticed that the tops of his ears had turned bright red.

"How about you, Suvester-Stallone?" said the one who was man-handling Mischa's shoulders. He had a buzz cut that made his head look like a cue ball and a faint mustache.

"Get a life, Sean," said Suvi.

"Who's your new buddy? Did anyone tell her she came dressed like the guy who sits in front of the LCBO?"

"Her name's Ana." Suvi rolled her eyes. "Ignore him, Ana."

"Charmed, I'm sure," said Sean. He'd started bouncing on the balls of his feet. He wore rolled white sports socks and black-and-red trainers that looked as though they'd smell of fish. "You've landed yourself with a pretty cool crowd here. Now that Fraser and Jack and me have turned up."

"And *I*," said Ana.

"What?"

"Now that *I* have turned up. Not *me*."

Sean recoiled as if Mischa had suddenly sprouted a contagious disease. "Jesus," he said. "You're even lamer than the fag and his hag."

"C'mon, bro."

"See you round, freaks."

"What was that?" said Suvi.

"What?"

"Correcting his grammar."

"He left, didn't he?"

"I guess so." Suvi turned to Mischa, who was folding away his notebook with a face like stone. "So, that's another thing, I guess: the jerks are jerkier this year."

"Suvester-Stallone isn't even that offensive," Mischa said. "It wasn't even that offensive when they were calling you SUV last year."

"If you let them get to you, they've won," said Suvi.

"Right," said Mischa. "I'll bear that in mind. See you guys later."

Ana watched him go until Suvi jabbed her in the ribs. "Five minutes," she said. "Bathroom break, then I'll show you to the science lab. If you get there too early, Doc Rutter will try and schmooze you over the periodic table. Phoebe told me that the guys in this school are all pervs, especially the old ones."

———#———

Ana waited for the electric buzz before heaving her shoulder against the gray metal door.

Inside, the center smelled of cinnamon, and as she entered the waiting room she noticed an incense stick smoking gently on the reception counter. From behind a mountain of papers, Becca glanced up and flashed a sympathetic smile.

She didn't have to say anything for Ana to understand: still no news.

———#———

The first Mennonites came to Canada from Europe where they were being persecuted for their beliefs. The ones from Chortitza, in Russia, arrived in the 1870s and came to be known as Old Colony (Altkolonier) Mennonites. At first they liked life in Canada, but after a while many of the Old Colony communities started to feel they were being pushed around all over again, mainly because the government wanted them to send their children to English-language schools. So in the

1920s some of them moved to Mexico and Paraguay. In the 1960s, a number from Peace River, in Alberta, went to Bolivia.

Ana read what the scribe had written for her. The scribe was an ESL teacher who floated between classrooms, helping the kids with learning disabilities and writing tests for the odd person with a broken arm. Her name was Miss G, and she sat with Ana in third period to help with Ana's written homework. Ana planned to begin seeking her out during gym class too—especially on those days when her class was supposed to be playing dodgeball or basketball or anything that meant wearing gym shorts rather than sweatpants.

Miss G's writing was large and loopy, and Ana found it strange seeing the words that she'd dictated, haltingly, rendered in fluid, flawless prose. The only writing Ana had done at school in Bolivia had been copying from the Bible. Never before had she seen her own ideas written down on paper like this.

Tell us a bit about YOU! said the worksheet handed out in history class that morning. *Research your family's culture (Chinese, Métis, Scottish, Bangla, etc.) and describe it in the space below.* "Extra points for illustrations!" their teacher had enthused. "We'll display our cultural mosaic on the board at the back of the classroom for all of grade nine to see."

There are approximately 15,000 Old Colony Mennonites in Bolivia, most of them farmers. They mainly speak Low German, or Plautdietsch, except for the men who speak a little Spanish to do business with the locals. They believe in peace and consider violence a sin. Unlike other Christian groups, Mennonites don't baptize babies but wait until a person is old enough to decide for themselves if they want to be baptized. Old Colony Mennonites tend to be more conservative than other Russian Mennonite groups. They are very religious and they live by specific rules to limit the use of technology and contact with the outside world. For instance, tractors can be used for farming but must have steel wheels so they can't go on the roads.

Alone in the library, Ana flipped through the open encyclopedia at her elbow. There they were: a Mennonite family, formally arranged in height order.

Old Colony Mennonites believe that girls should be married by the time they reach about twenty, and most families have six or seven kids. Boys leave school by the time they're fourteen, and girls when they're between eleven and thirteen. Then the girls help their mothers and the boys help their fathers. Not all Mennonite communities are so strict. Konferenz Mennonites usually complete high school, and the girls don't have to cover their heads.

Ana closed the encyclopedia and read back the last section of her paper.

Where I'm from, this is how you would recognize an Old Colony Mennonite kid: A boy would be wearing dark blue overalls and a shirt buttoned up to the very top—maybe a white shirt, or maybe a plaid one. A girl would be wearing a kerchief over her hair, and if you could see her hair through the scarf it would be pulled tight in two braids. She'd be wearing a long dress with long sleeves and an apron over that, and a straw hat with a wide brim for walking to church or school.

She picked up her pen.

It's better there.

"Hey, I've been looking everywhere for you." Suvi landed in the chair next to Ana and began zipping up her pencil case. "No one works in the library on a Friday afternoon—especially not in the first week of school."

"This is for our next class."

"Exactly. You've got all weekend to do it. Come on—we'll get stuff from the corner store on the way home."

—⁂—

My *might-have-been* life. My *should-have-been* life. How different everything would be if my family had chosen differently before I was born: my accent, my clothes, my friends, whether or not I liked math, what sort of food I'd eat when I was sad, how I'd cut my hair, if I'd read for fun, how interested I'd be in visiting other places.

I would have grown up near Winnipeg, because that's where my father's family were from. Perhaps by now I'd paint my nails and try a cigarette if someone offered it to me and listen to music on headphones and look bored.

I'd have a mother *and* a father.

Colony Felicidad

On the way to their new life in Bolivia, my mother's father was given a copy of *The Complete Works of Shakespeare*. According to my Aunt Justina, who was about my age at the time, he got it from a traveling salesman whose car had broken down on the side of the highway. My grandfather had done something or other to make the car work well enough for the salesman to get to the next town, and in gratitude the salesman gave him the book.

"No one's buying Shakespeare these days, anyway," the salesman had said. "Next week I'm going into beauty products instead. Housewives will pay a handful for beautiful skin."

My grandparents are all dead now. My mother's father went first, then her mother, then my father's mother, then his father. By the time my mother disappeared, it was just my parents and me and Justina. That's a pretty small family by Mennonite standards.

The Complete Works of Shakespeare sat on a bedside table in my parents' bedroom. My father isn't much of a reader, so I guess it was my mother who kept it out. There weren't many books in Colony Felicidad, and most of them were written in German. So an English copy of *The Complete Works of Shakespeare* was a bit of an enigma. You could almost have mistaken it for a Bible, because it was that fat with a dark blue cover and gold lettering on the spine. Perhaps because it looked a bit like a Bible imposter, my father always seemed to regard it with suspicion. Nevertheless, the one time he caught me starting to open it—my hands still traced with flour from rolling tortillas in the bake house—he swiped it out from under my fingers as if it were a baby he was pulling from a fire.

"Run along," he'd told me. "And wash your hands."

As I'd left I watched him return it tenderly to its place, and I wondered if he knew that the salesman had said no one wanted Shakespeare any more.

Toronto

POLICE STATIONS IN BOLIVIA were often small storefronts with POLICIA NACIONALE hand-painted over the doorway. The last time Ana had been in La Paz, many of the local stations were boarded up because the police were going on strike. The police station across from Walpole Secondary School was different: all glass and aluminum and concrete, with a shiny municipal sign in English and French outside and a wheelchair ramp next to the steps.

Suvi had been the one to mention the police. She'd watched a TV show about unsolved disappearances that provided a phone number to call if you had any information that led to their resolution. She couldn't remember the phone number but, she'd told Ana, in most cases you'd just call 911, anyway, or report to your local station.

None of the women Suvi described from the TV show sounded like Ana's mother. Ana had seen missing-person posters in the airport at Santa Cruz, and the few times she'd joined Suvi on the subway here, there had been faces and descriptions of missing people on the screens overhanging the platform. Ana had studied them for traces of Helena Doerksen, to no avail.

There were no officers standing guard outside the police station on Walpole Street on Saturday morning. Mustering her courage, Ana heaved open the front door and walked into the atrium. It was cool and quiet. A man sat behind a tall information counter, the top of his head bobbing in sight as he moved back and forth between piles of stapled documents.

"Hello," Ana would say. *"Can you help me? I'm looking for a missing person."*

Or, *"Please, is there someone here who can help me find my mother?"*

There was the sound of a chair being scraped back as the man behind the desk stood up. He was young, probably still in his twenties. Italian or maybe Greek. His hair was gelled and combed back in waves. He picked up a paper bag from the edge of the desk, peeped inside and rolled it up again before shoving it into a drawer with a grimace.

His lunch, thought Ana. *Did his mother pack it for him? Or his wife? He looks too young to have children—*

"Can I help you?"

Ana stared at the badge on his chest. Was he a real police officer, or just a secretary? He didn't seem to have a gun holster—

"Miss?"

"Yes?"

Her father: what would he say if he knew she was here?

If this had been such an obvious thing to do, why hadn't he done it already? Then again, perhaps he had. Perhaps the police had her mother's case already in hand. If Ana started poking about now, perhaps they would get suspicious . . .

A girl arriving in the city with her father, out of the blue—

"Can I help? Are you looking for someone?"

The police can find out anything, Suvi had said. *The government is spying on us all the time as it is. All of our information is already out there. The only difference is that the police have the tools to locate it and piece it all together.*

They could do this. They could find her mother. Starting with this man standing in front of her right now, watching her with a funny look on his face as though he was trying to work out if now was one of those times they told him about in training, when he'd have to remember a good head lock and his other defensive maneuvers—

"I said, can I help you?"

And then they'd find her, and Ana would have to find the right words to say to her—and would that make them a family again?

What if her mother didn't want to be found?

"Miss?"

Ana swallowed.

"I'm sorry," she said. "I got the wrong place. Sorry."

French classes were divided into two streams: regular and advanced. "Stupid and smart," as Suvi put it on Monday morning when they got to school. She could say this because she was in the regular stream, like Ana, who had never learned French before.

"You're not stupid," Ana told her, rankling. She was still digesting the news that there were yet more new teachers she would have to meet: a different one for every subject, apparently. How would she remember them all? Every time a bell rang she jumped and her mind went blank. Would it always feel this way, like school was just a process of being jolted from lesson to lesson?

"I'm stupid at French. I can't make out any of the words when the teacher is talking—it just sounds like one long stream of mumbo-jumbo." Suvi pulled Ana close. "Thing is, it doesn't matter . . . because the grade nine French teacher is Hot. As."

"Hot as what?"

"You'll see."

Mr. Peterson ("*Tom* Peterson," whispered Suvi—"he supplied for us a couple of times last year . . .") wasn't exactly young. His hair was peppering gray at his temples, although it was still thick and a little wavy on top. There were creases at the corners of his eyes even when he wasn't smiling. Blue eyes. A hawkish nose and a thin, smirking mouth. He seemed to bounce a little as he walked, like a kid with too much energy. He wore pants that could have been jeans but were too dark to tell; they probably just squeaked through the staff dress code. His tie was knotted loosely; the top button of his shirt was undone. ("He's got a tattoo," said Suvi in Ana's ear, touching her chest just above her heart. "Here.")

He wore two rings: a gold band on his left hand and a silver band of interlinked bones on his right index finger. Dropping a stack of worksheets on a desk at the front of the room, his hand sliced through a shaft of sunlight, and the bones glinted.

"Take one and pass it back." He scanned the register. "Ana Rempel?"

Ana raised her hand.

"Hi, Ana. I've been told you're a recent transfer. Some kids have all the luck." He smiled quickly. "Done any French before?"

"No."

"That's not a problem. Follow along as best as you can for now and see me after class."

The bookshelves in most of the other classrooms were generally only half-filled—and then with plastic-bound teaching manuals, rolled-up wall charts, pads of graph paper and dictionaries. In Mr. Peterson's room, books were squashed into every available inch of shelf space, sometimes two or three deep, lined up vertically but also stacked sideways on top. Some were new, but most looked a little tatty and curled in the corners. Ana tipped her head sideways and squinted to make out the names on the spines. *Proust. Camus. Foucault. Sartre. de Beauvoir. Cocteau. Genet.*

"So, Ana."

The classroom emptied quickly as soon as the bell rang, and Ana stood awkwardly by the teacher's desk. She could hear Suvi laugh in the corridor outside with a girl from their homeroom.

Mr. Peterson snapped his briefcase closed and sat on the desk, hands folded in his lap. "Bolivia. Tell me about it."

"I'm sorry?"

"Do you miss it?"

"No. I mean, yes. A bit. It's very different."

"Heard of a book called *Papillon*?"

"No."

"I know French Guiana's a long way from Bolivia, but it's the only country in South America where they speak French. It's about this guy who's been wrongly convicted of murder and escapes from a penal colony there called Devil's Island. You should try it in English first—I could lend you my copy. Only if you're interested. It's not on the syllabus."

"Thanks."

"OK, so that's the fun stuff. Here's the necessary stuff." He pushed a workbook toward her. "Conjugations. To be, to have, and to do. *Être, avoir, faire.* Learn them for the end of the week—we'll run through them after class. And a vocab sheet. At that rate, you'll be caught up before the end of term. I'll bet you could be in Miss Simon's class within the year."

"OK. Great."

"Don't sound so excited." Mr. Peterson grinned, heaving himself off the desk. "Welcome to Walpole, Ana. I know it feels like it now, but it's not a life sentence."

———#———

Faces are one thing; names are another. The names at school are a jumble to Ana's ears, and she is too shy to test them on her tongue. Arman Mouradian, Narek Ishmaeli, Davit Seferjan, Crystal Gao, Melanie Xhang, Danton Washington, Kwame Aziz. Those are just the people who sit in front of her in homeroom; she's embarrassed to turn to look at the other faces as hands are raised during attendance.

At lunch, Suvi tries to help, but her attempts to conjure people from the names elude Ana too. Brodie Thomas is into parkour. "You know, free-running," says Suvi. Ana nods. She does not know.

Michaela Freeman always asks for extra credit assignments; she's already decided that she wants to go to Yale. Mason Keeler can solve a Rubik's Cube in under a minute. Sam Foster is a fact machine on anything to do with planes. Max Klaas is a pothead but he plays the ukulele really well, even when he's stoned. Jaimie Leung is still into Pokémon.

Then there are the groups. Skaters, jocks, drama geeks, hot Asians, Asian nerds, Banglas, Somalis, druggies, ADD kids, punks, goths, preps, gender benders, techies, cool honors kids, dorky honors kids, band geeks, arty kids, straight-up nerds . . .

"Why so many groups?" Ana asked. Even in Colony Felicidad she had been an individual at school, known first as the student with the best penmanship and later, as she grew older, as the teacher's helper tasked with helping the little ones with their letters and reading.

"Human nature," shrugged Suvi. "It just seems strange to you here because you're new and on the outside. But I bet there were groups in your old school too."

Ana drew breath to disagree—of course there hadn't been: their school had been too small, they had all worn the same clothes, half of the kids there had been related to each other, no one there had heard of goths or punks or LGBT or manga or ADD . . . but then she stopped.

"There were a couple of mean girls," she said. "And the 'good boys' and the 'bad boys'—that's what our parents called them."

"I bet the grown-ups had groups too," said Suvi. "You probably just didn't notice them because little kids don't think to look for that sort of thing. You assume grown-ups are all the same."

Ana nodded so much that she wondered if the bones in her neck would wear out. She sipped milk from a carton and poked a piece of breaded, fried white meat that was probably chicken into a pool of red gloop that probably once had a passing relationship with a tomato. Usually she brought lunch from home, but today Suvi was treating her. She wondered if Suvi had a point about the grown-ups.

—⁂—

In the school library there was a section labeled "English Learners." It included books printed half in English and half in Arabic, or Chinese. There were books with CDs in plastic envelopes taped to the back cover. There were counting books, rhyming books, large print books. There were also some picture books, which were really meant for little kids but offered a comforting safe space away from vocabulary lists and learning targets.

Ana discovered a book called *A Bear Called Paddington*. It was about a little bear who travels from Darkest Peru all the way to London, England, as a stowaway on a boat. He eats marmalade and is very polite. When he finds himself at a big, busy train station, he waits behind a bicycle rack until a kindly couple notice him. They decide that they can't leave him there all alone, so they bring him home where their two children bathe him and feed him hot buttered toast and listen to his stories about life in the jungle.

It was a story that made Ana smile on some days and double over with a gnawing loneliness on others. She loved Paddington and pitied him and envied him all at once. She veered between identifying with Judy, the girl who looked after Paddington, and Paddington himself, because he was foreign and easily confused by things.

She made sure never to let Suvi see her reading a book meant for little children.

—✦—

There were two counselors working in the guidance office. There was a doctor too, who came in twice a week, and a nurse who had yet to encounter a malady that couldn't be cured with Tylenol. On the wall outside the guidance office were four plaques with their names: Mrs. White and Miss Perigee to the left of the notice board, Dr. Mitchell and Nurse Jacobs to the right.

The only other person in the school who had his name on a plaque was the principal, Mr. Vasquez, and that didn't hold as much fascination for Ana. It was seeing the women's names that made her pause. Mrs. White was old enough to be someone's grandmother, with an enormous bosom and gold-capped teeth, but there was her name etched in metal for the whole community to see. Miss Perigee couldn't be much older than Maria, yet there she was too.

Miss Perigee had asked to meet with Ana to make sure that she was settling in at school. Waiting to be called in to her office, Ana studied the posters neatly pinned around a big framed photograph of a tree blossoming with smiling faces.

Thinking about suicide? read one. *Think of us first.* Beneath an image of a girl staring out a rain-streaked window was a phone number in big block numerals.

Drinking and Driving: A Lethal Mix read another. *Save a life: Call a cab.* Here too a phone number.

How about *"Looking for your mother who you last saw in Bolivia almost ten years ago, who's now somewhere at large in the second biggest country in the world and you don't even have a phone?"* thought Ana. That would be a good one.

There was a whisper of a raincoat brushing the door as a tall woman strode in through the waiting room, satchel slung across one shoulder. She smiled at Ana as she passed. The keys were already in her hand as she approached the door to the doctor's office. A casual turn of the handle, and she had disappeared inside.

That wasn't the nurse, thought Ana. Nurse Jacobs was short and squat and sharp-tongued. Then, realization dawned: the tall lady in the raincoat must have been Dr. Mitchell. Ana had assumed that Dr. Mitchell must be a man; there had been no women doctors back home, and Mitchell . . . well, now she thought about it, there was no reason that Mitchell shouldn't be a woman's surname as well as a man's. How stupid could she be?

"Ana?"

Miss Perigee had stuck her head out of her office door. *How long had she been waiting there? Had she called Ana's name once already?*

"You were miles away," she said, as Ana gathered her things. "Come on in."

———*⁂*———

Waiting for Suvi outside the basketball court, Ana counted the purple ribbons that still remained on the fence running the length of the block. There must have been fifteen, originally—when Faith Watson first went missing—one for every section. Now there were nine.

A little blond boy careened into view, and Ana watched him jitterbug down the path toward the swings. He might have been three, more likely two, but steady enough on his legs to run pretty fast. When he tripped on a crack in the pavement, Ana jumped to her feet.

The older girls in Colony Felicidad were like mothers to all the little ones, whether or not they were siblings or cousins or just neighbors, so Ana's first instinct was to rush to pick him up, to brush the grit from his scarlet knee and smooth his sweaty head with her hand.

She stopped short of doing so, though, standing lamely by as a nanny appeared with a stroller and another child, cooing and chastising the boy by turns, pulling a wet wipe from the stroller pocket and dabbing at the graze while his howls dwindled to sniffles.

Invisible, Ana sat back down on the bench. Suvi had had to explain the concept of a nanny to her a few weeks ago. ("Babysitter" had been another new word: when Ana told Suvi that her parents would happily leave her, at four years old, alone inside the house while they went to work outside nearby, Suvi had nearly choked on her drink and said something about calling social services.) This nanny was Asian, maybe from the Philippines. Suvi and Mischa had shared a Filipina nanny as toddlers, apparently. Her name was Wendy, and she had left her three children and her husband to travel halfway around the world to look after foreign children.

Ana watched the little boy reach for his nanny's hand and pull her on toward the swings. The nanny was wide-hipped and moved slowly, with a calm, gentle lilt. She was smiling, but her gaze seemed somewhere far away. *Was she thinking about her own children,* wondered Ana. *About the mother that she would like to be to them?* Ana's thoughts drifted. *Whose fault was it that this woman was here, and not there, at home? Someone must be to blame, but who?*

The nanny had stopped by the iron fence and now seemed to be considering one of the purple ribbons. She tested it between her fingers as if to prove to herself that it was real. Then, splaying her fingers, she widened the loops and pulled the tail ends straight. Ana watched her touch her knuckle to her forehead, chest, and each shoulder—left, right, left—before turning to call the little boy.

That was when Ana realized that she had no right to feel irritated. The nanny hadn't left *her.* Presumably, coming all this way to look after someone else's children was the only thing she could do for her own. Like the Central American families they had just read about in social studies class, who put their children on trains to Mexico, to the United States, just so they could escape being recruited into gangs. Not knowing where they would end up, hoping for the best. Desperate, but also somehow noble, that sacrifice.

Had Ana's mother made a similar one? Her mother, who had left in the middle of the night and lived here for ten years without so much as a letter sent home?

What kind of mother did that, without a very good reason?

"Turn your head a little—*that* way," said Mischa, showing her with his pencil.

They were sitting in Suvi's room. Suvi was painting her toenails, and Ana, despite teasing from the others, was still trying to finish her French homework. Mischa was using a sheet of graph paper to sketch Ana's portrait.

"You really don't have to," Ana said.

"Yes, Meesh, you do," interjected Suvi, blowing on her toes. "Ana, trust me, you'll love it."

Ana looked down at the worksheet in her lap, trying not to move her head. It hurt her eyes, trying to read like this. She already had a headache, and although she didn't like to say anything, Suvi's room felt hot and airless. The smell of nail polish wasn't helping.

"Can we open a window?" she said at last.

"Sure. Hey, do you guys want something to eat? There's sushi in the fridge. Julie got this bamboo mat and all these crazy little bento accessories from the Japanese supermarket and we've got, like, *kawaii* stuff coming out of our ears down there."

"Great!"

"Ana?"

"I'm not hungry, thanks."

"If you say so. I'll be back."

When she had gone, Mischa looked up at Ana and paused.

"Do you ever take your hair out?" he said.

"Excuse me?"

He reached over to give her braid a playful tug, and she flinched. Something about that brief moment of contact made her shiver. She didn't fancy Mischa in *that* way—plus, she suspected he wouldn't be interested anyway—so the chill she had felt wasn't all bad. And he was smiling. "Is it, like, really, really long?"

"I guess so." Ana felt herself grow even hotter. She swallowed dryly. It hurt her throat.

"Can I see? I've finished the drawing already."

"Uh . . . *jo*, OK." She untied both bands and loosened the coils with her fingers until her hair fell in loose curls down her back. Back in Colony Felicidad, a girl without braids would have been considered as good as naked, and she knew she was blushing.

"Wow. Jeez, Ana, you should let it down like that for school." Mischa flipped open a fresh page and began sketching. "It's, like, Pre-Raphaelite."

Ana swallowed again. The room had started to contract to a beat. Her temples throbbed. Just then, the door opened and Suvi came in.

"Whoa," she said when she saw Ana. "Your hair!"

"I know," said Mischa. "Here, look."

He handed Ana the first sheet: a delicate profile in gray pencil tracing her high forehead, the clean line of her nose, slight overbite and long neck. Her ears were small, her eyes large and solemn. He had spent the most time on her braids—hundreds of hatch marks against the straight line of her center parting—and ended the sketch at her collarbone.

"It's beautiful," she said. Then, "Can I keep it?"

"Of course. Here, this one too." He handed her the second sheet. This sketch was more vague, and he had cheated on her face—he had drawn her smiling, although she had felt too weak all afternoon to smile much—but it showed her hair falling over her shoulders like an avalanche of silk.

"Oh, my . . ."

"See what I mean?"

Suvi came over to look too.

"Mischa, you're amazing."

"I know."

"Hey, Ana, have you finished your French yet?" Suvi's smile began to fade. "Dude, you're really pale. Are you feeling OK?"

"I'm fine. Maybe a drink of water?"

"There's a cup in the bathroom."

---#---

She hid the pictures in her math binder, which she shoved in her bag under the bed as soon as she got home. Just as well, as the room was dark by the time she heard her father calling her.

"Ani?" He felt her forehead with the back of his hand. "Why didn't you call me?"

"You weren't home. I fell asleep." Her throat felt as though it was stuffed with cotton wool. "It hurts here."

"I'm calling a doctor—no, no, you stay put."

---#---

It took less than a day for the news to spread through her class.

Ana's got mumps.

What?

Mumps. We won't get it because we were vaccinated.

Only kids in third world countries get mumps.

My dad says if she wasn't vaccinated for mumps she wasn't vaccinated for measles, either.

You know kids die from measles?

I hope they've locked her up somewhere safe.

The doctor gave her painkillers for the pain in her neck and head and told her to drink lots of liquids. The swelling under her ears on either side of her face would go down in a few days, he said. For now, she'd just have to get used to looking like a hamster and get as much rest as she could.

That evening, a note dropped through the letterbox from Suvi:

Sean's telling everyone you're delirious and seeing monkeys and you've started saying you're the Wrath of God. Don't worry, I punched him when I heard. He's such a douche!

The Wrath of God had something to do with a movie Sean's brother had shown him by a famous director called Werner Herzog. Ana remembered the name because she had to tell him it was pronounced *Verner*, not Werner. The movie was about a group of *conquistadores* traveling down the Amazon River in search of El Dorado, led by a tyrannical madman. They all end up either shot by arrows, or starved, or delirious with fever, and in the final scene their raft is overrun by monkeys and the madman keeps saying, "I am the Wrath of God!" and promises to found a pure line of rulers with his own daughter and reign over the continent with her.

For some reason Sean thought this was really funny and he'd taken to whispering "Wrath of God!" whenever Ana was nearby. "Dodged any poison arrows today?" he'd ask her in front of his friends. She'd told him that the Amazon didn't actually go through Bolivia, but Sean didn't seem to care.

Ana rolled onto her side. No matter how much water she drank, her mouth remained as dry as sandpaper. She closed her eyes and counted the throbbing in her temples: one-*two*, three-*four*, five-*six* . . .

There is a long table, set with goblets and salvers, in the middle of a field. Scrubland: dry, yellow, studded with prickly pear. Wine topples from one of the goblets, staining the ground red. A vulture has landed; it grabs a piece of bread with its talons, enormous wings beating hard. Plates smash, the tablecloth tears. Another vulture, and another. They are enormous, black with white ruffs around their necks, like the noblemen in the old painting reproduced outside the history classroom at school. Their heads are bald, flat, and the rough skin is a dull pink.

With hooked beaks they tear at the meat, working in greedy silence. They will have spotted the table from afar, drifting on motionless outspread wings high overhead, circling, circling anything that might be carrion. Farmers in the eastern lowlands dread them. They can strip a cow of its flesh in minutes. Sometimes they go for days without eating, then they gorge.

Through the open bedroom door, Ana could hear voices downstairs: her father's and another man's. She could tell by the rhythm and cadence of their speech that they were speaking Plautdietsch.

You can see on her birth certificate, here, her father said. *You see, parents' names—there, and there.*

Miloh. Helena.

Sometimes she went by Lena, you said?

Yes.

More words, obscured by the movement of bodies and shuffling of paper. They walked from the kitchen to the front hallway. *Don't go,* she thinks in a haze. *Don't leave.* If her father left, she would be totally alone in this strange city, this strange country. Totally alone in all the world.

Dankscheen.

Bitscheen.

She lapses between the voices and her dream. The vultures at the table, feathered old men, Papa at the door saying, "Come, Anneli, we must go quickly," and Colony Felicidad receding behind them, smaller and smaller until it is a blur on the horizon, evaporating into nothingness on the trembling, arid air.

—#—

A week later, Suvi dropped her backpack on the floor and sat herself at the foot of Ana's bed.

"Feeling better?"

"Yes. Much."

"You look better." She reached into her bag. "I'm supposed to give this to you and say not to worry about getting it all done before you come back. It's just to keep you in the loop. Readings, worksheets and stuff." She paused, her mouth curling into a smirk. "And you have a message from Hot Tom Peterson."

"What? Why?"

"He told me to tell you that he hopes you're feeling better really soon and that he's looking forward to seeing you in class again." Suvi blew theatrical kisses. "He's *pining* for you, Ana."

"That's stupid. He didn't say that last bit."

"You'll never know, will you?" She zipped up her bag. "So, I was going to ask you last time, before you got all sick and weird on us . . ."

Ana watched Suvi look around the room, and didn't have to try very hard to imagine how it seemed to her.

"Yes?"

"Your mother. How's the search going?"

Ana shrugged into her pillow. "It's not. Not for the last week. Not even very much before that."

I don't even know if I want to find her. I had a chance, at the police station—

"You tried Google?"

Ana nodded.

"What about chat rooms? You know, like asking real people?"

"I don't know how you do that."

"First, you have to find a chat room. Like, if you were looking for a Star Wars geek, maybe you'd try a sci-fi chat room. Or, I don't know, one for aspiring poets if you knew she wrote poetry. People know people. This city is a lot smaller than you'd think."

———#———

Sunday night at the library is a quiet time. Not so much at the front desk—people often come in at the last minute to return books before the week starts—but further back, at the work stations and in the children's section and between the stacks.

Ana told her father she had to look something up for school the next day. She said she would be an hour at the most.

She went to the computer farthest from the others and typed in "chat room." Those had been Suvi's words. It would need narrowing, though. "Canada," she typed. And then, "Mennonite."

This was OK. She wasn't involving anyone else by doing an Internet search—not the police, not the people at the Women's Center. Ana could remain anonymous. If someone came back to her with information, she could take her time deciding what to do with it.

The first result to appear was something called MennoCanTalk. These would all be liberal Mennonites—ones who used computers and drove cars and let their kids wear jeans to school—so how likely could it be that one of them would have any Old Colony contacts? She clicked the link to a home page that listed a handful of active discussions and scanned the topics. *Best Bible camps? Divorce and the divided house. Prayer requests. Anyone heard from Fran in Kelowna?*

Those were just the ones that people had commented on most recently. In the upper corner there was a search box.

"Colony Felicidad," she typed. *0 results*, said the pop-up.

"Helena." *0 results.*

"Bolivia." Two threads: one discussing a rape case that had been in the news the year before, the other asking about mission work.

What did she know about her?

"Berliner doughnuts." One thread: *Does anyone have a good recipe for plum butter?*

"Lennon Sisters." She clicked on the sole result. *Favorite oldies?* asked someone with a cartoon cat as his avatar.

My grandkids have just discovered the McGuire Sisters, he'd written. *"Sugartime" and "Goodnight, Sweetheart, Goodnight"—nice clean lyrics. I told my daughter to put them on to Patti Page. Any other suggestions for family sing-alongs?*

Halfway down the page, something caught Ana's eye: a two-sentence reply from someone who called herself Perdita.

Show them the Lennon Sisters on YouTube. We watched Lawrence Welk reruns as kids and I always wanted to be Janet.

Ana clicked on the avatar: a gray square that the poster, Perdita, hadn't bothered to customize.

About: *Lapsed Menno*
Threads I'm On: *Favorite oldies?*
                           MennoCan Book Club
                           First Light Congregation, Toronto—experiences?

Colony Felicidad

Cayua means "the ones from the forest." The Bolivian Guaraní used it to describe those indigenous people who the early Jesuits failed to convert. Nowadays it means anyone who fails to integrate.

In the days when the Guaraní were hunted by slave dealers, they could either hide in the jungle and take their chances with their bows and arrows against the slave dealers' guns, or they could join the Jesuit missions. Then the slave traders started to target the missions too: on any given Sunday, when everyone gathered for Mass, it was easy to capture many Guaraní at once. For this reason, some Guaraní returned to the forest to be *cayua*. Perhaps that's why they don't find it strange that the Mennonites in Colony Felicidad also prefer to exist out of time and place.

Agustín was the Guaraní driver who used to take shipments to Santa Cruz when we had more cheese than we could sell in the local town. His pickup was twice the size of one of our wagons and he called it his third baby. Twice a week he would park at the end of the long driveway that connected the campo to the main road and wait for one of the boys to arrive with a wagon rattling with milk cans. Once a week he came for the oranges and avocados that grew in our orchards. If the boy was late with the wagon, Agustín would toot the horn and the little kids would fight over who got to commandeer one of Papa's horses down the driveway to greet him.

Sometimes he gave little presents to the children: carvings, usually, because he was good with a knife and as a driver he spent a lot of time waiting around. It might be a slingshot for one of the boys, or a rattle if there was a new baby. Once he carved a figure of a man who was a priest looking one way, and a devil looking the other.

Like many peasants, he chewed coca leaves as a habit—one cheek bulging with a ball of screwed-up leaves that he drew from a woven pouch worn around his neck. Every now and then he'd take a pinch of *lejia* powder from a sack kept in his back pocket and add it to the wad in his mouth. One of the boys told me that this ash powder was what made the leaves work, in the same way that adding baking soda to vinegar is what makes it fizz. People in Bolivia chew coca like people in other parts of the world drink coffee, and Agustín loved it more than anyone.

There was only one time that I got to speak to him, because Klaas Epp's father saw a group of us girls gathered around Agustín's pickup in our flowery dresses and straw hats with the dark ribbons and he made quite a scene at the community meeting that night. Normally we wouldn't have stopped to speak to a man who wasn't a relative, but we had been walking back from the dairy when Agustín pulled up alongside us and said he'd drive us the rest of the way home. There wasn't anything improper about it, but I suppose Klaas Epp's father wasn't to know that. It was me, Susanna, her sister Maria and their little sister Eva.

Agustín was telling us about *pombéro*, the forest spirits. He talked to us in broken English because our English was better than his German, and our Spanish was non-existent. From what we could gather, the most feared *pombéro* was the hideously ugly *Yasi Yateré*, whose feet faced backward and who kidnapped children by trapping them in climbing vines. Parents would leave honey for him in parts of the forest known to be dangerous—for instance, where the river was deepest and the undercurrent strong. Then there was *Cuarahú-Yara*, who whistled like a bird to lure young boys out on egg-stealing missions.

"You tell your brothers to stay out of the jungle or *Cuarahú-Yara* will get them," he said, before hooking a finger around the wad of coca leaves and shifting it to his other cheek.

"What about us?" asked Maria. "Or is he only interested in little boys?"

You could tell by the way she said it that she meant Agustín to hear the question differently. I don't know how else to describe it, but it was as if Susanna and Eva and I weren't there anymore. Agustín's face crinkled into a grin, but before he could reply, Klaas Epp's father had appeared at the end of the drive, shouting at us to get home.

He must have had a pretty serious talk with the Guaraní driver after that, because from then on Agustín hardly dared look at us girls, let alone start up a conversation or offer us a lift in his pickup. Never again did he venture onto our driveway; he'd always stop on the main road and the boy with the wagon would have to haul the milk tanks or the oranges and avocados or the cheese and tortillas right up to the top of the slope before Agustín would jump out of the driver's seat to help with the loading.

He was back to being *cayua*, as were we. And the forest, now that we knew it to be populated by spirits plotting our destruction, was more unknowable than ever.

---#---

The long driveway that linked Colony Felicidad to the main road—the one where Agustín never dared to drive his pickup after that time with Maria and the talk about the forest *pombéro*—was just one of several wide, dusty roads that crisscrossed Mennonite land in our corner of the country. Every now and then you would see a small airplane buzzing low in the sky, shaving the tops of the trees as it hummed over the forest before disappearing we knew not where. The nearest airport was Santa Cruz.

Later, we learned that the planes were using our quiet community roads to land and refuel. Sometimes a truck with a Paraguayan licence plate would drive through too, although in neither case did we ever talk to these people responsible for what technically could be called trespassing. No one seemed to question it or make much effort to come up with any explanation. Maybe it was just that most of us didn't think that way. We were taught to work hard and mind our own business, and that's mostly what we did.

It's hard to mind your own business when a plane crashes barely a mile from where you live, though. It's hard not to feel the impact that sends a row of straw hats leaping from the coat hook by the door, brushing the ground below with a dry whisper, and not glance around the schoolroom to find everyone else looking just as startled. It's hard not to let out a yelp of surprise when every slate covered in carefully chalked German letters hits the floor with an echoing clatter. It's hard not to notice the tiles cracking under your feet from the aftershock or the uneven glass panes rattling in the window frames and everyone holding on to the long, white school desks as if, no matter what happens, those desks will be the last thing on earth to move.

Some of the boys rushed outside to see what had happened, but our teacher barricaded the doorway with his arms to prevent us girls from following. We watched the boys lope away from us through the pampas grass, their lean bodies crooked with haste, as a twist of smoke drifted over the distant tree line.

When school ended at lunchtime, we heard how a wheel appeared to have got stuck in a ditch as the plane attempted to land, tripping it into a cartwheel. Diedrich Pankratz said he saw a truck driving away from the wreckage with two people in the back. There was no one in the plane, which by some miracle had not burst into flames.

We kids trailed the police team that came to investigate at first light the next morning, while the sky was pink and the grass still weeping. It was one of those rare times when it helped to be considered a child: the adults thought we were too young to see anything we weren't supposed to, or at least too young to understand it if we did. We hovered in clusters, the boys venturing nearer the forest, the girls loitering around a bandy tree trunk fifty yards back. It was a hot, still day, and the little ones soon took off their headscarves to flap at the cloying air. We saw the police emerge from the trees and register us, a flock of blond-braided girls, bare-legged, holding up fluttering cotton squares as though we were waving good-bye to lovers at a train station.

"They took the bit of the plane that records its route," said Bernhard Hamm, breathless in his determination to be the first one to report back. "The box bit."

"The police?"

"No, the passengers who went off in the truck. They took it with them. And the log book too. The police are angry as bulls."

The plane had a Paraguayan registration, but no cargo. The police thought it must have been landing to collect a shipment from the waiting truck. When the plane crashed, the driver must have taken the pilot and passengers away along with whatever it was they'd come to collect.

"A shipment of what?" I asked.

Of course, I had to be the stupid one. And as usual, it was Maria who seemed to draw out my stupidity.

"Coca, dumdum," she said.

By now both her father and Klaas Epp's dad had come out to meet the police. Gerhard Buhler waved his daughter over.

"Take the little ones inside," he told Maria. He tipped a nod in my direction, and for an instant I sensed that he was going to tell me to come with them to stand by the police car. But he didn't. That wouldn't have made sense.

Toronto

Hi.

Ana's fingers hovered over the keyboard.

I hope you don't mind, but I think you might know me.

She stared at the avatar's gray silhouette, the pixels in the name Perdita blurring on the fuzzy screen.

My name's Ana. It changed when I left Bolivia. I think you might be Helena. Or Lena. Or maybe something else, but if those names mean anything to you that won't matter.

She unscrewed her water bottle and gulped deeply. An older woman sitting at the computer opposite frowned over her spectacles at her before resuming her own search. Ana replaced the bottle cap and hesitated.

Papa and I are here, in Toronto.
If you want, you can write to me at ananeli@mymail.com
If you're not who I think you are, I'm sorry for bothering you and hope you will delete this.
A
P.S. Justina told me about the Lawrence Welk thing. I still have your note and your pearl necklace.

———⫯———

They went to the Baptist church because it was closest. The service was unlike anything Ana had experienced before: guitars and drums and clapping and swaying and laughter in the middle of the sermon. It felt like a party.

When they emerged onto the street, her father said, "Don't worry, we will find another church. There are churches here for people like us. I'm sure of it."

As they walked, a woman emerged from a house a few doors down, carrying a small dog under one arm. She was fussing over one of its paws and had to push the front gate open with her hip. Ana's father held it for her and she smiled.

"Thanks," she said. "He hates these boots, but his paws get filthy in the park. His nails were a mess the last time we went to the doggy spa. Mortifying, right?"

The dog stared up at Ana and her father with doleful eyes. Each of its paws had been squeezed into what looked like a pink rubber balloon. The harness it wore was dotted with a daisy print.

"Have a good day," said Ana's father, and closed the gate for the lady as she coaxed the little dog down the sidewalk.

"I've seen ones like that before," he said to Ana in a low voice, once they had turned the corner. "They're everywhere here. They treat their pets like people. What good is a little dog like that to anyone? It doesn't chase rats or herd anything useful. It wouldn't frighten a child, let alone a burglar—and besides, their owners have expensive security systems."

"Perhaps she doesn't have children," said Ana. Her father grunted.

"You never wore boots like that," he said. "What is a spa, anyway?"

Colony Felicidad

A few weeks before we left, I lay in bed early one morning listening to the sound of wild dogs crying at the fading moon. I was thinking of the chickens locked up in their shed and wondering if they connected the dogs' howls with their own hair-breadth mortality. The chickens were safe, but only because they were locked up. Eventually, some of them would get eaten by the people who kept them from the dogs. It wasn't much of a life.

I was half asleep when something landed with a thud on the roof right about my head. The walls shuddered as I jolted upright. There was a dragging sound that crossed the room, then another thud on the ground outside.

I would have gone to the window, but I was too frightened of what I might see. I thought of the jungle *pombéro,* of *Yasi Yateré* with the backward feet and swirling vine traps, and I pulled the blanket up to my ears.

Another thump, louder this time. Something landing from a height. Then a faster drag, screeching down the shingled roof.

Thump.

Thump.

This was the longest silence yet. Whatever it was on the roof, it was staying put this time. I stared up at the ceiling until my eyes went funny—until I could almost believe that I was seeing through the plaster—and then I edged myself out of bed and crept toward the window.

Footsteps, then, retreating from the other side of the house, and a single person, certainly no more than that. I leaned out of the window and craned my neck. I could see nothing on the roof. For a second, I was distracted by the beauty of the dawn sky—so many colors!—and it was because of that that something struck my cheek as I hung out of the window. Something warm and wet. I touched my cheek, and I saw that my fingers were stained. The early light wasn't bright enough see what color, but I didn't need any light to be quite certain.

My fingers might have been dipped in strawberry jam. But of course it wasn't jam that now ran in a slow, thick trickle down the side of our house.

———

Frank Reimer came banging at our door a few minutes later to say there were vultures circling our house. His sister had spotted them on her way to milk the cows, flying low with their enormous wings spread out wide as sawhorses.

When he and Papa and a few of the other men ran at them with waving arms, the creatures flapped and fussed, refusing to be frightened away. That was when Frank realized there must be something drawing them to the roof.

Papa got there first, and almost as soon as he did, he shouted at me to stay inside. From the kitchen window, I watched Frank and his brother climb up a ladder that someone had set up against the outside wall and listened to the scuffle of their feet overhead as they hauled something—*draaaaaag-THUMP* . . . *draaaaaag-THUMP*—to the edge of the roof.

By now several of our neighbors had come out to see what was going on. My father asked for someone to bring a tarp, and one was rustled out of a shed somewhere and laid out on the ground beneath the bit of roof where Papa and Frank stood. I didn't want to watch, but even though I knew whatever was coming was going to be bad, I couldn't look away. I thought Papa would shout for me to go to my room, or close the window—that there would be some warning— but he must have been preoccupied because all of a sudden there it was, dropping onto the tarp with a thud and a cracking noise that made the others outside gasp.

It was a wild dog, or it had been. Its jaw was hinged open to show a long black tongue, like an eel or a monstrous slug crawling out of its mouth, and the tawny fur at its neck was stained a reddish brown where its throat had been slit. Its long hind legs were crossed at the ankle but its forelegs had splayed as the body fell, so it looked as if it was reaching up for help. Its mane was puffed, frozen in alarm. It wasn't as big as some of the dogs we'd spotted prowling on the *chaco* plain, sizing up our chicken sheds, and its enormous ears made it look more like a fox than a wolf. My stomach churned as I felt my fear turn to pity.

"Its hip was crushed first—maybe hit by a car," someone said.

"But its throat . . ."

"To put it out of its misery?" my father suggested. It sounded halfhearted.

"On your roof, Miloh?"

I opened the kitchen door and edged onto the step, thinking that everyone would be clustered around the other side of the house. I was wrong. Gerhard Buhler stood a few paces away, his back to me, using a piece of straw to pick his teeth.

"What a thing, eh, Anneli?" he said, without turning around. "Poor old Milobo." He dropped the straw and walked around the corner to join the others.

Milobo. I hadn't heard that name for a long time. Some of the Spanish workers used to call my father that, years ago. In their language, *lobo solitario* meant lone wolf.

I went back inside, locking the door behind me.

Toronto

THREE DAYS, AND NOTHING. Two days of checking her email, and an extra day when Ana couldn't get to the library because Suvi insisted on dragging her to a Dance Crew tryout after school.

"Lame," said Mischa. "I thought you played real sports."

"I do," huffed Suvi. "I can do this too."

"To get guys to notice you."

"Not true!"

"Whatever."

"You've got the legs for Crew," said Suvi to Ana, when he'd gone. "And the hair. If you ever take it out of those braids, that is. Honestly, Ana, braids are for third graders."

She was joking, Ana knew. She told herself this.

The reality was, the thought of dancing in public terrified Ana. She didn't even know how to dance; it wasn't an instinct for her the way it seemed to be for these kids. It was something other people did, something suggestive and a bit wrong and also kind of silly.

"Karen Spelberg is Crew vice-captain this year, so she gets to help Miss Kaplan choose the squad." Suvi rolled her eyes. "Karen totally only got chosen because her sister was captain three years ago and her dad's company sponsors the costumes. A monkey could dance better than she does, but she hides it by bossing everyone else around."

"I'm going to look ridiculous," said Ana.

"Everyone will be too worried about themselves to notice you. Honestly, ninety percent of the girls who try are awful. *I'll* probably be awful, but I promised Julie and Steve I'd give it a go anyway. Steve kind of dared me."

"So how is me being there going to help?"

"Moral support, duh!"

They were put in different groups almost as soon as they arrived. Ana could tell that Suvi's was the preferred group: athletic girls, keen girls. The ones in Ana's group were the geeks who thought they could dance, the wannabe cool girls and over-confident loudmouths. Ana stood at the back and marked the steps without actually throwing herself into it, and no one seemed to care. They were taught the words to a cheer for an upcoming basketball game, which was easy enough because it was just call and response. Putting the words and the steps together was another matter—but when the time came for her group to perform, Karen Spelberg didn't even bother watching them fumble their way through it. She was too busy teaching a new routine to the preferred group.

"It's kind of a Lady Gaga tribute," she was saying, and Ana saw Suvi roll her eyes.

"Callbacks on Thursday," they were told at the end.

"That was the stupidest thing ever," Ana said as they walked home.

"You were OK," said Mischa, who'd hung around to watch the last five minutes. "You were actually keeping in time."

"No I wasn't," Ana said. "I can move my feet, or say the words, but I can't do both at once. What is even the point of it?"

What is even the point?" laughed Suvi. "Dude, you sound like us. You're becoming real Toronto."

"Wonderful," said Ana.

"What's not to love? You can get a 416 tattoo now, like Drake."

"You know you love us," said Mischa. "You know you love it here."

"Gimme a T! O! R! O! N!—"

"You're giving me a headache," snapped Ana.

"Whoa. What crawled up your butt and died?"

Mischa snorted.

"You think Toronto's great because everyone's always saying it is," Ana said. "But that's only because they've never been anywhere else."

She'd surprised even herself. But then, in the seconds it took to speak, a feeling she hadn't known she had assumed its ugly form.

"Just because people tell themselves it's great doesn't make it so," she continued. "They go on and on about how tolerant everyone is here, but that's only if people behave the way you expect them to. You're not tolerant just because you eat at ethnic restaurants. This city is neither here nor there. It's like an awkward teenager *trying* to be cool."

Both of her friends stared at her, and she realized that it was unthinkable to them that someone should suggest that this wasn't the greatest place on earth, a beacon for the huddled masses of the world. Maybe because for them Canada didn't mean frozen pizzas, soggy fried chicken and casseroles like cat sick in plastic microwave containers.

"And it's ugly," she continued, even though by now she wished she could take it all back. "All those big apartment blocks. Gray and flat and concrete and it just goes on and on and on. Even the nice bits. All those fake fancy houses and the fake beach—"

"Come on, Mischa," said Suvi with a hard look. "Next thing you know, Little Miss I'm-Too-Good-For-This will start calling us fake too."

As they went, Ana pretended to ignore Mischa's doleful backward glance. It made her ashamed to punish him; he didn't know how to wound and he wounded so easily.

"No tarrying after school on Friday," her father said that night, as Ana peeled the plastic from a tub of potato salad about to pass its expiry date. "We're going away this weekend."

Ana's fingers froze over the tub lid. For some reason, her mind flitted to the purple ribbons tied up and down the street.

"Only for two days," he said. "We'll come back on Sunday."

"Where are we going?"

"To visit friends. Family, actually."

"Mama?"

Her father turned away from her and filled his glass with water from the tap.

Colony Felicidad

Here, just about everyone was family. It was sort of a joke among Mennonites, because the community was so small and self-contained, but it's the kind of joke that you can't take too far or people start to get offended.

Most of our neighbors were cousins or second cousins or, if they weren't, then their grandparents were, or maybe their great-grandparents. Sometimes I'd see a glimmer of Susanna in the corners of an old woman's eyes—watering eyes, maybe, behind thick spectacles, lined with crow's feet—or the curve of my father's mouth in Frank Reimer's smile. At a distance, the little boys could have been almost entirely interchangeable with their white-blond hair, crinkling blue eyes and freckled, upturned noses.

But being family doesn't stop evil from creeping in.

There were rumors, a long time ago, of things amiss in Wilhelm Penner's house. Whispers among the women when his wife and three daughters turned up at church one morning with four black eyes between them. The eldest daughter became pregnant, even though she wasn't married, but she lost the baby just a few months in. More whispers—*Terrible to say, but it's probably for the best*—but it wasn't until my mother's father stood up and insisted that the elders do something that anything happened. There was a lot of tension around that time, Justina later told me: her father had been the only man to bring the whispers out into the open, and it embarrassed some of the elders so much that there was almost a falling out. But at last a meeting was convened by the church leaders. They brought Wilhelm before three ministers, who between them got to decide on the punishment for his crimes. The ministers were the most powerful people in the colony, elected for life and entrusted to try any colony member for any crime apart from murder. Those ministers heard the charges brought against Wilhelm at a trial attended by all the male members in the colony, the worst crime being that he'd made his own daughter pregnant. If he'd been excommunicated, he'd have gone to Hell; as it was, he begged forgiveness and was allowed to stay. His wife's uncle arranged marriages for the younger two daughters then and there, and that got them out of his house. The eldest daughter went to live with cousins. No one talked about it after that. Most people probably figured that if God had wanted to intervene further, He would have.

Sometimes, I can't help but wonder if God occasionally falls asleep on the job.

Toronto

THE NEXT MORNING, Ana didn't bother waiting for Suvi to walk by her house. Instead, she went early to the library, logged on to a computer and waited.

No new messages.

She Googled "MennoCan Book Club" and scrolled through pages of discussions about books she'd never heard of. There were four pages of threads, some of which ran to fifteen or sixteen pages each, where conversations had grown heated. She tried to search for posts just by Perdita, but this only worked page by page, and there were too many for Ana to go through so laboriously.

She returned to Google.

"First Light Congregation Toronto," she typed. There it was: a website, an address. The church building was an old brick Victorian affair with a modern addition that looked in need of some sprucing up. But the faces on the page about language classes looked friendly, albeit nothing like the faces Ana remembered from Colony Felicidad.

About Us, History, Contact, Gallery. Ana hovered the cursor over the gallery page and clicked. Six albums: *English School, Summer Fair, Meet the Team, Choir Trip, Junior Cooks, Bible Study.* She clicked on an image of a man wielding barbecue tongs and grinning broadly.

Most of the faces were close-ups, with a few group shots. Ana scrolled past thumbnails of the aerial snaps—too little detail—and the shots of children and men. She clicked on a few of the shots of women, some of which opened in another window and some of which wouldn't.

She scrolled on. Stopped.

Ana leaned forward so that her nose was almost touching the screen. It looked like a picture of herself, but as far as she knew no one had taken her photo since she'd arrived in Toronto. Besides, the hair was too dark, and loose. But the nose that she'd always felt was too big, the way one eye squinted more than the other when she smiled . . .

She clicked on it.

This page cannot be displayed.

She returned to the gallery page. There, in a pixelated square the size of a matchbox, was a picture of a woman who might be her mother.

"Or not," Ana said. She tried tilting the screen, double clicked. Still the same error message. Her heart drilled in her chest.

It has to be. Is it? Is that you?

———#———

In History, Suvi sat next to a girl called Katie Stamper. Ana caught her eye and smiled. *I've seen her,* she wanted to say. *I can show you. I'm pretty sure it's her!* But Suvi seemed not to notice and turned the other way.

Suvi didn't join them at lunch. Mischa ate in silence, grunting in response to Ana's attempts at conversation. He said he had to leave early for an art club meeting.

Suvi and Mischa emerged together from a different door at the end of the day, leaving Ana waiting outside their usual exit with her backpack hugged to her chest. When she saw them rounding the corner without her, she called out to Suvi. A backward glance, a death stare, something whispered in Mischa's ear. They quickened their pace, leaving her there.

———#———

"This is as bad as it gets," said Mr. Peterson.

He was standing by his car, grinding a cigarette butt into the tarmac with his heel.

"Excuse me?"

"Other kids. In a couple of years they'll stop wasting so much energy being mean. Everyone will get on with life again."

"Um . . . ok."

"For now, you should make the most of being fourteen. No bills, no mortgage, no snotty-nosed kids needing feeding and clothing and permission forms signed and lifts to the mall. You have all the time in the world to listen to music, read books, watch movies. Start figuring it all out while you have the time. Your brain's forming all these crazy pathways right at this very second. You can make them stretch further now, in a way you won't be able to when you're older. It's what you'll have to work with when you're forty and up for the same job as a fat guy with coffee dribble stains on his shirt."

"OK."

"No, not *OK*. Say 'What the shit have you been smoking, Peterson?'"

"I thought it was just a cigarette." Ana dropped her bag on the ground.

"Got any plans for this weekend?"

Going to visit some strangers that might know where my mother is. "Not really. What about you?"

Mr. Peterson looked surprised to be asked.

"I don't know," he said at last, frowning as he nudged the cigarette butt with his toe. "I haven't thought about it yet. Usually it's my wife who makes the plans."

"Is she away?"

"We're separated."

"Oh. I'm sorry."

"It's better. Less arguing. More time on the weekend to do nothing."

"Right." Ana nodded as if she knew what he meant, as if she'd been a high school French teacher with a car and a smoking habit and an estranged wife too. "Could I borrow that book you mentioned? It's not in the school library."

"*Papillon*? Sure. I can bring it in for you on Monday." He took his bag from the hood of the car, pulled out a set of keys. As he moved

Ana caught the faintest suggestion of cigarette smoke, a breath of it glancing off his skin, coloring the air with his smell.

"I'd wanted to read it this weekend." She swallowed. "My dad and I are going away."

Mr. Peterson nodded. "OK," he said. And then, "OK. I, uh . . ." The parking lot was empty. A group of kids came out of the gym exit, talking loudly as they cut across the field to the road.

Mr. Peterson turned back to her. "We could get it now. My place isn't far from here." He unlocked the door. "Hop in."

They drove south, toward the lake, past squat brick houses with beer-belly porches. The porches were an affectation, Ana decided, since they actually prevented light from coming in through the front windows. Inside, the houses would be dark, even the south-facing ones.

A bridge took them across an enormous valley, a green gash in the middle of the cityscape. Other cars glided past them, fast and smooth and soundless. Mr. Peterson told Ana that he'd spent entire summers in the ravines as a kid, building forts and collecting golf balls that had washed downriver from the golf course. He and his friends would sell them back to the golfers for twenty-five cents apiece. The ravines were dark and cool even on a sunny day, a relief from the hot concrete and glaring glass downtown.

"Once, my pal Rocky and I built a raft and floated it all the way down to the viaduct," he said. "Like Huck Finn."

"Who?"

"You've never heard of Huckleberry Finn? C'mon, Ana!" He shook his head and smacked the steering wheel. "God, if our mothers had known half the stuff we got up to. We weren't supposed to play in the ravines, period."

"Why not?"

"Because in their minds the ravines were filled with rabid coyotes and poison ivy and pedophiles. And what if the river flooded?

And what if one of us broke a leg down there and no one heard our screams . . ."

"That sounds unlikely."

"It does, doesn't it?"

They had reached the neglected fringes of the harborfront, where the lake met industrial yards and empty parking lots. In the distance, the islands nodded their bushy heads.

"What a waste, eh?" said Mr. Peterson. "Paris has the Seine. London has the Thames. Even Vancouver has the freaking Pacific. We've got a perfectly decent lake and some sweet islands, and look what we do with it. *Nada*. Screw you, beauty—that's what this city is saying. We just go from un-space to un-space and live in the bits in between."

"I kind of like it. There's space to think. Nothing here tells you *what* to think."

Mr. Peterson looked at her.

"OK," he said. "I'll give you that. And ugliness has its own beauty, I guess."

It felt strange, hearing her teacher talk about beauty, and Ana hoped she wasn't blushing.

"Why do you still wear your ring, if you're not living together?" she asked.

Mr. Peterson blinked, but kept his eyes on the road ahead. "We're separated," he said. "Not divorced."

"What's the difference?"

"It's not permanent." He corrected himself. "It *might* not be permanent. And taking it off feels like throwing away a big part of my life. Ten years, almost."

They'd stopped in front of a building that looked as if it had once been a factory. In front of the main door, spindly trees stood to attention in large barrels. The windows were long and anonymous and stared blindly across the expressway. Ana had never known someone who lived like this: in a big building with other people on floors above and below them. People with different families, different languages, different-smelling food, different religions, all packed in together. Like a prison, or a hospital or a boarding school.

"This is it. I'll leave the car here—it shouldn't take me long to find *Papillon*, and then I'll drive you home."

They took the stairs up to the second floor and followed a corridor lit by flickering strip lights to the far end of the building. Brass numbers were screwed to the painted door. Inside, the loft was mostly empty: two white sofas and a floating kitchen counter, a glass coffee table and a desk with a dining chair pushed against it—the seat clearly too high to fit underneath. There was a rolled-up newspaper on the counter and a mug next to a book splayed facedown on the coffee table.

"Cool," said Ana, because she felt she ought to.

"Most of my stuff's in boxes in the bedroom. Give me half a sec."

When he returned, she said, "The furniture isn't yours?"

"This stuff? No way. It belongs to my landlord. Like I said, it's all in boxes."

"You should change things around. Move the sofa so you get light from the window. And bring the desk here so that you can sit at it properly. Have the chair by the counter instead . . . where do you eat?"

For a moment Mr. Peterson looked sheepish, like a little boy who had been caught chasing ants with a magnifying glass.

"I order in a lot. Usually I eat in bed and read."

Ana nodded. "But then your room will smell like takeout," she said. She saw that he was embarrassed. "I know, because I do the same. My dad can't cook, and we don't talk much, so I eat upstairs sometimes. Or at Suvi's."

"Right." Mr. Peterson looked around the room, nodding to himself as he mulled her suggestions. "OK," he said. "Let's do it. Give me a hand with the sofa?"

When they had finished, Ana said, "Will your landlord mind?"

"Who cares? In fact, I think I might make a habit of staying in hotels from now on just so that I can change the furniture around for the heck of it. Like *The Borrowers*—oh wait, let me guess, you haven't read that one, either. Anyway, the place works better now. You were right."

"It could use a little color." She unzipped her backpack. "Here. We had to do a Moroccan table for United Nations Day. Suvi got it from the dollar store—she won't mind." *It's not like she's talking to me, anyway.* "I'll say I must have dropped it somewhere."

The shawl was thin, woven with cheap, crinkly gold thread, with green and white beads knotted into the tassels. She draped it over the back of the sofa.

"Now you can pretend you live in a souk," she said.

"Or a harem."

"A what?"

"Never mind. It's nice. Thanks." He gestured to the book on the counter. "We'd better get going. Traffic going north is a drag this time of day. Your dad will worry."

"No, he won't. He assumes I'm at Suvi's. I think he prefers it that way."

Mr. Peterson straightened one corner of the shawl. "In that case," he said, "I didn't have time for lunch today. Do you like dim sum?"

———#———

She told him about the *cayua* and about Tomas de Molli and Popi and Sue. What it was like trying to figure out a new country all alone.

"We're learning about the settlers in history," she said, plucking a spring roll from the sweating foil box. "We have to choose a person who had to do with settling the New World and make a poster. Like Jacques Cartier—only I think someone's taken him already."

"Do Virginia Dare," Mr Peterson said, and disappeared into the bedroom. He emerged a minute later with a comic book and handed it to her. She brushed the grease from her fingers and examined the cover. *Daughter of the New World* read the title in outrageous bold letters. Beneath it, a picture of a girl in a white nightdress carrying a torch through a dark forest.

"Can I borrow this?"

"Sure. Just don't cut it up for your bristol board. It's from the sixties. Belonged to my big brother." He scraped the last of the fried rice onto his plate. "I should probably return it some time."

"Thanks. It looks better than my last project."

"The essay about your family?" Mr. Peterson smiled. "I guess you kind of walked into that."

It was the photograph of the girls in braids and hats that had done it. One of Sean's friends had drawn mustaches on them during lunch break, not minutes after the reports had been posted on the classroom wall.

"Children of the Corn! Children of the Corn!" Sean had howled after her in the cafeteria, while Fraser Kwan and Jack Thurloe pelted her with sweet corn from the salad bar. Since then, there had been daily jibes about Bibles and quilting, wagons and polygamy. Most of their references meant nothing to her, and that somehow made it worse.

"How are your folks finding it?" asked Mr. Peterson. "It must be even harder for them, in some ways."

"My father works all day," she said. "He says if his hands are busy his mind is peaceful." *I worry every time he leaves the house that something will happen to him, that he won't return.*

"And your mom?" Mr. Peterson stifled a belch, clasped his hands behind his head and leaned back on the sofa. He'd long since untucked his shirt from his jeans.

An image flashed into Ana's mind: the woman at the barbecue. Her nose, her squint, her hair dark and loose. The image that led nowhere, to a dead end. *Page expired.*

"She's dead."

She hadn't needed to say that. Why had she said that? Had she wanted him to feel sorry for her? Mr. Peterson's hands dropped to his sides and his face slackened.

"Oh, Jesus. I'm sorry, Ana."

"It's OK."

She was acting, and she knew it. *Dead* had never meant anything; it certainly didn't feel of anything. But Mr. Peterson didn't know that. Ana looked down at her lap. A moment later she felt the sofa cushions shift beneath her as he leaned forward, placed a hand on her shoulder.

"Was it recent? Is that why you came here?" His voice was soft. Outside, the sky gleamed black-blue as a bruise. There were tea lights on the coffee table, and their reflection shone like fireflies in the tall glass windows.

"In a way." She forced herself to look at him. His hand remained on her shoulder. "It's OK, really."

He nodded. Then he cleared his throat, and she felt his hand lift from her shoulder.

"I thought you said you were going away this weekend," he said. "If that's the case"—it sounded as if perhaps he didn't believe her or, perhaps, as if he hoped it wasn't true—"I should take you home."

"I can get the subway." *Stop it, Ana. Stop being pathetic. What are you doing?*

"Don't be silly—it'll take as long to drive you to the station as it would to get you home. Just past Monarch Park, you said?"

"Yeah."

"I'll box up what's left and you can take it back for your dad. I'll bet it'll be just what he fancies after a day at the coal face." He reached for the piled takeout boxes. "You can tell him you ordered these at Suvi's, OK?"

———*——

Something about the paper—the yellow hue and rough edges, the deep, irregular imprint of the type—felt as though it belonged to someone else. Her name looked awkward in the box marked "Infant." That had been her: an insentient, mewling, burping grub wrapped in toweling, cradled in her mother's arms. The other names seemed equally foreign. *Miloh Abram Doerksen. Helena Alma Doerksen, née Rempel.* Who had they been? And what had happened to Anneli Marie Doerksen?

Ana looked at her father, sitting in the seat opposite and staring out the window at the flat, green countryside sliding past. *Toronto-Fallowfield-Aylmer*, their tickets said.

"Why do we need this?" she asked, lifting the birth certificate.

"As identification. Proof of who we are."

"Is this about Mama?"

"They are family. They or their neighbors may be able to help us find her."

Ana chewed her lip. She was too close now to tell him. Let him find her his way. She would get to her first.

"Do you think they're looking for us?" she said at last. "Susanna and Justina? Frank Reimer?"

"They are there. We are here." Her father looked at her quickly, then away. "I like to think they are praying for us."

The man who greeted them at the station had a red face and heavily whiskered jowls, a slumping belly straining the suspenders on his breeches and brown hands the size of spades. He led them through a small parking lot past SUVs and camper vans to a quiet lane where his pickup was parked.

"Johan is your mother's cousin," said her father.

"Our mothers were cousins," corrected the man, heaving himself into the front seat. "On the Rempel side."

He didn't speak much, this Johan, although he whistled as he drove them onto a main road.

They turned down a rutted path that reminded Ana of the driveway to Colony Felicidad, where she used to sit with the older girls selling lemons and limes. Here, the bushels were filled with apples and squashes, the last of the summer corn and bundles of dried lavender.

"I hope you're hungry," said Johan. "Katherina's been cooking since Thursday."

The Rempels had four children: a girl and three boys. Elizabeth, their daughter, was the eldest.

"I'll be fourteen in April," she told Ana, as the family sat down around the long kitchen table.

"I'll be fifteen in July," said Ana. "So we'll both be the same age for three months."

This seemed to please Elizabeth. She kept cutting glances at the green bandana Ana had used to cover her head, but whether they were looks of judgment or envy Ana couldn't tell.

They said a silent grace and then Katherina rose to help their guests to a meal of roast chicken, mashed potatoes and green beans. Slices of yellow dairy butter were lifted onto steaming wholemeal buns that Katherina and her daughter had baked that morning. A pumpkin pie was cooling on the windowsill, and tall jugs of lemonade sweated condensation on the tablecloth. Ana noticed her father eyeing the spread as if in a dream and felt a sudden pang of guilt.

"Eat as much as you like," said Katherina to Ana with a kind look that nevertheless made her feel self-conscious. *Tall girl*, Katherina was probably thinking. *One more growth spurt and she'd be as tall as Johan. Good thing I don't have to feed her.* "I'll make up a hamper for you before you go. Usually I'd freeze the extras but you should take them home with you."

"Thank you," said Ana.

She did not know how to talk to these people. Her people. It should have been easy, but why? They were strangers to her, their customs the rituals of a faraway place. She ate in silence, listening to the adults make safe, polite conversation that skirted the real reason for the visit. Even now, Ana wasn't entirely sure what that reason was. She waited until the men had finished eating before bowing her head in another silent grace. Then she helped Elizabeth to clear the table.

"Why don't you show Ana the barn?" suggested Katherina, as the last of the dishes were brought in. "I'll bring you some pie later."

"They're only two weeks old, so they've got to stay with their mother. If you'd come a few weeks from now, I could have let you take one back with you."

Ana heard the kittens mewing before she saw them, squirming against their mother's sprawling belly, partly covered by a thicket of hay. Two were white and two were ginger, and it was hard to tell which paw, tail, or hind legs belonged to which, they were so entangled in their sweet-smelling nest.

"They're really cute. Are you going to sell them?"

"Papa says we'll have to. They'll be a nuisance otherwise. I'm going to give one to my friend, but we'll put a sign up for the rest."

"Which one will your friend get?"

"The little guy with stripes." Elizabeth pointed to one of the ginger kittens. "He's the runt, so no one else will want him. And that way he can still see his mother."

They watched as the mother cat began to wash one of the kittens, thoroughly but lovingly, ignoring the squeaked objections and licking its fur into punkish peaks.

"Mother says your mother and my father are related somehow. Why didn't she come with you?"

"We're looking for her. She's not here, though—she went to the city."

"Is she hiding?"

"I don't know." Ana felt the other girl's curiosity billowing. "Have you ever heard of Virginia Dare?" Elizabeth shook her head. "She was the first baby born in America after the settlers arrived. The colony where she lived was wiped out, but no one knows if it was a massacre, or if they all starved to death, or what. They just disappeared. And supposedly Virginia Dare was the only one who survived."

"But your community wasn't wiped out."

"No."

"I heard Mother say life is pretty hard down there." Ana frowned. "She said it's easier to stray off the path in a lawless country. We don't have so many temptations here."

"My mother didn't do anything wrong."

"I didn't mean that." Elizabeth blushed. "She said, knowing her parents, your mother must be a good person. Maybe she didn't run away for bad reasons. Maybe she was running away *from* them."

Ana decided then that Elizabeth wasn't so bad. She remembered the look on Suvi's face as she and Mischa left school without her, and suddenly she wished with all her heart that she could stay here, on this farm, with this girl for a friend.

The barn door opened behind them, and the girls turned to see Katherina balancing two plates on her arm.

"Don't let me interrupt," she said. "Come back to the house when you're ready."

———— # ————

It was early, still nighttime, when she heard the voices downstairs. In the bed next to her, blanket tugged up around her ears, Elizabeth snored softly.

Ana slid out of bed and tiptoed across the room. Through the crack around the door, she could tell that a light was on in the hallway. She tested the door handle, eased it open.

Padding toward the bathroom, she hesitated at the top of the stairs. Someone was sitting at the kitchen table—she could only make out part of a pajama leg—and someone else was at the stove, pouring coffee. She recognized her father's voice, so low that she could barely make out the words.

"So he told them?" It was Johan who was pouring the coffee. "He told the police about what happened in Moth?"

A pause, then the sound of a mug set on the table. "He did it to show he meant business."

Ana held her breath, straining to hear the rest.

"But the gun is at the bottom of the lake," said Johan. "Ten years. There is no evidence."

"There is if Gerhard decided to tell them. That's what he wanted me to know." Muffled words. Then, "He was furious with Agustín. Shot after him into the forest, said afterward that it was wolves, he was defending the livestock."

"You shouldn't have gone after him when he was in that state."

"No. But I did."

"Then what?"

"Agustín wasn't badly hurt, but his wife found out, naturally. Raised a stink and went straight to the police. When some officers turned up the next morning, Gerhard convinced them that he'd thought it was wolves. Paid some money to hush it all up. But he also must have said something about me to make them interested. They came back the next day, asked questions. If they had taken me, she would have been left with no one. So we had to run."

Ana crouched down to peer through the railing. Her father had his back to her. Leaning forward with his elbows on the table, he put his head into his hands.

"The dog was my warning. He told me he'd asked nicely, but there was only so much time before it would become obvious about Maria's baby. He needed my decision before that. I told him no. So, he thought he'd frighten me . . ." A sound that could have been laughter, or a sob. "We got it off the roof before she saw. But I couldn't protect her forever. After the police came, that was obvious."

"She's safe now. You both are."

"My daughter . . ." Ana swallowed. She had not heard her father sound like this before. "First to lose her mother. Then to lose everything she has known, to come to this place. Who knows what she learns at that school? You see the way the children speak and dress—"

"That doesn't matter. She is kind. She is intelligent. She is a good daughter. She will be fine."

"It's all my fault. One mistake, so long ago, and still now . . . I'm trying to makes things right."

"We know that."

Ana drew herself away from the staircase and scuttled back to Elizabeth's room. The black sky outside was turning silver, and she thought of the kittens in the barn: safe and blind and unaware that soon they would be taken away.

—#—

They departed soon after breakfast the next day. Ana sat in the back of the pickup with the hamper that Katherina had prepared balancing on her knees, while her father embraced Johan and exchanged good-byes. The boys were playing on the lawn, tumbling over one another like puppies.

"Come back and visit us," said a voice at her side, and Ana looked down to see Elizabeth smiling up at her. "Maybe next time you can hold one of the kittens."

"That would be great," said Ana.

Katherina came and squeezed her hand as the men climbed into the truck, and then Johan turned on the ignition and they were moving. Ana watched the girl go to stand next to her mother as they waved the visitors farewell. She watched them, two figures by a gate, waving, waving, until she could no longer see their smiles, and then she turned around to watch the open road disappear beneath her.

—#—

I'm sorry, she wrote. She folded the paper and sealed it with a rainbow sticker from a pad Suvi had left at Ana's house by accident, one she'd stolen from the teachers' supply closet. Ana waited until the water was boiling, then she told her father she was going across the street for five minutes. She would be back before the pasta needed draining.

There was no car in Suvi's driveway. Ana slid the note through her mailbox then turned and ran, as if the sound of paper brushing the floor might awaken a pack of sleeping wolves.

⸺ // ⸺

Her father brought the envelope into her room on his way to bed.

"This was under the front mat," he said. "I'm guessing it's for you."

There was a smiley face sticker on the seal, and a shooting star inside.

It's cool. Sorry for being a dick and making you try out for Crew. I didn't make it anyway. Thank God!

⸺ // ⸺

Halloween. Ana followed Suvi up and down front paths, hanging back as her friend rang bells and bellowed, "Trick or treat!" as she thrust her pillowcase into cobwebbed doorways. People smiled at Suvi, who had dressed up as a hobo: lumberjack shirt and dungarees, trucker cap and a shoe polish beard. They hesitated when they looked at Ana, trying to establish what she was meant to be—Suvi had given her a hair band attached to a plastic ax that looked as if it was half sunk into Ana's head—before wordlessly dropping fistfuls of candy into the EXPRESS PHARMA-CARE bag.

Coffee Crisps, Kit Kats, Hershey's bars, Snickers, Skittles, Mars, M&Ms, Butterfingers, Sour Keys, Twizzlers, Nerds . . . Oh Henry!

("*Nerds*," sniffed Suvi. "What do they think this is—1998?")

Up and down flagstone paths, cobbled paths, paved paths, pebbled paths. Up and down brick steps, wooden porches, concrete ramps, grassy slopes. Rubbing shoulders with devils and mermaids, disgraced politicians, astronauts, race car drivers, Rastafarians, hobbits, zombies.

"So?" Suvi asked her. "Pretty cool, right? We are totally too old for this, Ana, but no way was I going to let you miss out on the Halloween experience."

Ana nodded, aware of the ax tilting precariously on her head. "Some of the costumes are kind of . . ."

"Freaky? That's the point, Ana."

"It's a weird thing to celebrate, isn't it?"

"Dude, it's all about celebrating what scares you. It's, like, a really fun coping mechanism—with free candy. What's not to love?"

They divided their spoils in Suvi's bedroom—chocolate bounty for Ana, anything fluorescent for Suvi—before Suvi waved Ana across the street as she returned home.

"Sweet dreams!" Suvi called in a mock ghoulish caw. "Mind the vampires don't bite!" And then, just as Ana slid her key into the lock, "Oh, jeez, Ana—maybe lose the ax before your dad sees you?"

Colony Felicidad

If we worked hard and prayed hard, that would keep the invisible wall around our colony strong. Of course, bad things still happened; that was God's way of testing us. Like Wilhelm Penner, and the wild dog on our roof.

Sometimes the Devil wandered among us, tempting us to sin. Those were the times when the scent of sorghum hung heavy in the humid air, when the windmills clacked off their regular beat and the sunflower stalks bowed before the moon at night.

When blood ran down the walls and the retreating wolves left no footprints.

Toronto

AS USUAL, THERE WERE a couple of test messages from Suvi already open the next time Ana logged in. But at the top of the screen was something new: an envelope icon and a subject heading in bold letters.

RE: your message, it said.

Ana clicked on it before the panic could begin to flare up her fingertips.

Ani—if that's you?
What are you doing here? Can I see you?
My heart is dancing.
Mama

———#———

Suvi didn't eat cold cuts—not salami or ham slices or even leftover chicken—because she said the meat seemed too close to death. Stews were fine. Spaghetti Bolognese was fine. Pepperoni on pizza too.

"It's still meat, and it's still dead," said Mischa.

"But it's not *cold*," insisted Suvi. "Like it's been sitting in a morgue."

They were eating ham and cheese sandwiches at Mischa's house—Suvi had just made a show of picking the ham out of hers—and flicking through TV channels. Not that anyone was paying attention to the screen.

"Getting back to the *real* problem," said Ana.

"Right, right—sorry." Suvi grabbed the remote and switched the TV off. "We're going to be constructive. Mischa?"

"Maybe constructive isn't the thing right now." He looked at Ana. "Are you OK?"

"I'm fine."

"You're not, like, in shock? It's sort of a big deal."

"Mischa, Ana wrote to her *hoping* she'd reply. It's great news. Now we just have to make sure that this lady is who she claims to be." Suvi reached for a notebook in her bag. "Throw me a pen, will you?"

"Here."

"So, we need to come up with some questions that only Ana's mother will know the answer to. That way, we can test her."

"Like what?" said Ana. The fact that she hadn't thought about any of this sent a wave of humiliation through her. What *had* she expected to happen next? That, with the tap of a button on a library keyboard, everything about the last ten years would be made right again?

I could ask her to explain the things Papa was discussing with Johan, she thought. *The gun in the lake. What gun? Was it the same lake where Isaac Buhler nearly drowned?*

"Like, what pattern was on the curtains in your old bedroom? Or, do you have a weird birthmark that only she would know about?"

"She called me Ani in her message. That's what people used to call me in Bolivia."

"OK, but that could just be a fluke. We need more."

"You should write to her in your language, Ana—in German," interjected Mischa.

"That goes without saying." Suvi was scribbling furiously in the notebook. "Maybe something about your dad too?"

Ana tugged at a loose loop of thread in the rug by her feet. Right now, it felt like the only real thing in the room.

"There's the book he kept," she said at last. "It belonged to her. It came into the family by accident."

"Great! You can ask about that." Suvi tore the page out of the book with a flourish and handed it to Ana. "This would be a whole lot easier if they just microchipped people, right?"

"That's messed up," said Mischa.

"If they'd microchipped Faith Watson . . ." began Ana.

"They microchip condors that have been raised in captivity," said Mischa. "They leave one egg in the nest in the wild and take one egg for the lab. When the condors are born, they handle them with gloves so the condors don't get too attached to the people, and then after they're released they track them with satellites."

"Fascinating," said Suvi.

"Do the condors go looking for the ones that were left in the wild?" asked Ana.

Mischa didn't know, and Suvi wasn't interested.

"If you're both done with your morgue meat, we could get ready to go to Thandi's," she said. "Blow off some steam. Ana, you totally look like you could use some distraction."

"I'm ready," said Mischa.

"You're a guy—you can show up in jeans and a sweatshirt. Ana and I are going to make an *effort*." Suvi reached for her backpack. "Come on, Ana," she said as Ana began to protest. "Meesh, we're using your room."

—⚹—

Thandi Rosen was called that because her parents had met in South Africa in the '80s. Thandi was the name of one of their friends there; it meant "loved one" in Xhosa.

The first time Ana had seen Thandi, she'd had two white wires coming out of her ears. She was sitting on a bench outside the guidance office, fiddling with a small white box connected to the wires. Amid all the noise and motion of the hallway, she didn't look up when Suvi called out a passing hello.

"Is she mute too?" Ana had whispered to Suvi.

"Huh?"

"The deaf girl we just passed."

"Thandi's not deaf. She probably just didn't hear cause of her iPod."

"Is that her hearing aid?"

"Dude, she's not deaf. She's listening to *music*."

Thandi lived in a neighborhood of mansions and pool houses and massive landscaped front lawns. Miniature lanterns poked out of the rockery like glass toadstools along the path leading to Thandi's front door, which was guarded by two stone dogs. Through the cut-glass window it was possible to see bodies moving around each other in the hallway as people discarded their coats in a pile on the floor. The thump of music Ana didn't recognize resounded from another room.

"You made it!" Thandi flung her arms around Suvi and smiled at Ana. "Meesh, you look boss. Ana, I love your eyes. You should totally do them like that for school."

The eyeliner had been Suvi's idea. She wasn't going to bother with any herself, she'd told Ana up in Mischa's room—blue walls and duvet, pennants, a mug of something growing a crust on his desk, dimly lit, close and boy-scented, a book on the floor open to a picture of an abstract painting of figures in a bath—but she wanted to practice on Ana. "It's easier doing it for someone else," she'd said. When she finished, Ana's eyes looked bigger and older suddenly, staring back at her from the mirror. She'd let her hair down, but then felt so self-conscious she'd tied the sides back in a half-and-half. Suvi had grunted but said at least it was better than braids.

Thandi was handing out mocktails in plastic champagne glasses. The pink one was a Strawberry-Tini, Thandi said. "And this is a Virgin Mojito," she told Ana, passing her a green one with a mint leaf floating on top. When she'd moved on, Ana and Suvi exchanged drinks. Both were fizzy and tasted like ginger ale. Only the girls seemed to be taking them; all the boys Ana could see were drinking Coke.

"Sean probably spiked it with rum," said Suvi. "Or vodka, so it doesn't change the taste."

They worked their way around clusters of people into the living room. Ana perched on the arm of a sofa next to the sound system, while Suvi scrolled through the phone in the wireless dock.

Look out, this thing is gonna blow
I heard it from the people in the know . . .

"Do you recognize anyone?" asked Ana.

"It's mostly Thandi's sister's friends," said Suvi. "But there's Carter Fry and Ella Stephens. Bet you they're making out before this song's over."

I'm never going home
I'm running from the sun
Bullets at my heels
The devil's got a gun . . .

"What happens now?"

"We wait for people we know, or for one of the guys to get drunk. We could work the room, but everyone's older." Suvi finished her drink. "So what's up with you and Peterson?"

"What?"

"Nice try. You said he gave you a ride home?"

"Kind of."

"*Kind of*? Holy crap, Ana—"

"It's not what you think. He had to get this book from his apartment first—"

"You mean you went to Tom Peterson's *apartment*?" Suvi clapped both hands over her mouth. "What was it like?"

"Kind of empty. We had dim sum."

"He *cooked* for you?"

"We got takeout."

"And it took you until now to tell me any of this, *why*, exactly?"

"You only just asked now. And possibly finding my mother was *maybe* more important."

"OK, OK, true. Sorry."

Ana finished her drink. "Do you want another?"

"Yeah, sure. See if you can find some food too. Mischa said he could smell hot dogs."

Relieved to have escaped Suvi's questions, Ana slid off the sofa with a glass in each hand.

Rain is jumping up into the clouds
A girl has ceased to make her father proud . . .

—#—

By the time she got back to the sofa by the stereo, Suvi was drinking a Coke.

"So," she said, taking the bowl of chips from Ana. "Where were we?"

"I don't know."

"Peterson. Don't think you were getting off that easy."

Her voice seemed louder now; she was grinning.

"Is that spiked?" Ana said.

"I'm guessing yes, seeing as Sean was handing them out. Want some?"

"No, thanks."

"Don't be such a square, Ana. C'mon. For the team? For me? To celebrate finding your mom?"

"I've got this already. Maybe later."

"So . . . ?"

"So, nothing. Honestly, I've told you everything."

Suvi nodded sagely. "Look, Ana, I know. Older guy and all that. Have I ever told you about my cousin Alexander?"

"I don't think so."

"He's English. He's actually more like my second cousin, or my cousin once removed or something. He's just started university. Leeds. Like the soccer team, right?" She draped herself along the back of the sofa, propping herself up on her elbow so that she was speaking just behind Ana's ear. "Super cute. Sandy curls, piercing eyes, nice nose. Is aqualine when it's straight or bumpy?"

"I'm not sure."

"Anyway, it's a bit bumpy but in just the right way, you know? And this mouth that's, like, a bit stern, like Captain von Trapp in *The Sound of Music*—but in a good way too. And he's always saying such smart things, and he never wastes a single word, and when he talks to you, you just feel so damned special it's *insane*."

Ana looked around to see if anyone else was listening. She wondered where this was going.

"I must have been, I don't know, ten or eleven the first time. We were watching TV in his parents' basement—he was, like, fifteen, maybe?—and it was kind of cold because English houses are pretty drafty, and it was winter because we'd gone over for Christmas. So, we're sharing a huge chunky blanket, and suddenly our feet touch. And I think this is weird and I start sweating, but he just makes some joke about the movie and so I laugh it off. And then later our hands touch under the blanket. And that was all. Until the next year, it's the same thing, only it's not just our hands touching now . . ." Suvi giggled into her wrist. "It becomes like this weird habit, only it's just once a year, and just in his parents' basement, and there's always this huge chunky brown blanket, and neither of us ever says anything about it. Nothing else happens, even though I keep thinking it's going to."

"And?"

"That's it. This year he probably won't even be there because he'll be backpacking around Europe with a bunch of hot girls his own age." Suvi looked into her Coke. "Go on, finish it. It's gassing me up like a balloon."

Ana took the cup and smelled it. Then she drank, swallowed. Felt nothing.

"Want another?"

"Sure."

———※———

The night got better after that. Thandi came over with some of her sister's friends, and Ana found herself answering questions about vultures and police chases that wound up in Moth and how to chew coca. She didn't mention Low German or the way Susanna used to pull her braids so tight it made her head ache. Soon she was only talking about things that she had heard secondhand from Susanna, or Frank Reimer, or Agustín, but it didn't matter because they were listening. Suvi kept filling her glass and saying, "See? See? What did I tell you?"

Help me I know not what I see
I'm a stranger to the face looking back at me . . .

Justin Cook was there among them. Boy-band Justin, Suvi called him, because there was another Justin in their class who was a coding geek who played Minecraft all the time. Minecraft Justin was not at the party. Boy-band Justin was Karen Spelberg's boyfriend. He had a ski tan, a moody sweep of dark hair and the shoulders of an eleventh grader.

He wanted to know how to say something in *Plautdietsch*.

"*Goo'ndach*," said Ana. "Means hello."

"Something better than that," said Justin.

"*Das Leben ist wie eine Hühnerleiter: kurz und beschissen*," said Ana. She had read it once in a High German book borrowed from one of Agatha Bartsch's older brothers. "Life is like a chicken ladder: short and shitty."

"That's good," said Justin. "What about 'fuck off'?"

"People use the Spanish," said Ana, feeling her color rising. "*Tu madre*."

"*Tu madre*," practiced Justin, just as Karen Spelberg appeared behind him with his baseball jacket. Her eyes were wide and blue but slightly too close together, and when she didn't know she was being watched her top lip puckered in a way that made it look as if she was stuck in a perpetual near sneeze. "Let's go," Karen said. "This party's lame."

"*Tu madre*," said Justin.

"What did you say?" Karen looked at Ana and back to Justin as some of the others in the group started to snigger.

"I said, *tu madre*," said Justin, catching Ana's eye and winking.

Karen said nothing and walked away.

"Get this girl another drink," said Justin. "So she can teach us some more crazy shit."

— // —

Mischa's dad drove her home. He must have dropped off Mischa and Suvi first because Ana was alone in the back seat when she saw her father appear in the doorway, the kitchen light on behind him.

Mischa's dad opened the car door, offered her his hand. "Here we are, Ana. Got your bag?"

He followed her up to the front steps, hanging behind just a bit as her father edged aside to let her in.

"Good night, Ana. Mr. Rempel."

Her father said nothing as she went upstairs. A long time seemed to pass before she heard the front door close.

— // —

By the time she woke to his knock, the midday light was already glowing through the curtains.

"Are you unwell?"

She squirmed under the covers. Her head felt as if it might explode.

"I'm fine. Just tired."

"I have to go to Mrs. Fratelli's. When I get back, I want the house spotless."

"Yes, Papa."

"The boy whose father drove you home last night—who is he?"

"Mischa. He's Suvi's friend. A good boy." She swallowed. Her stomach roiled. "His parents look after old people with no families."

"They're Christians?"

If she closed her eyes, the room would stop moving. "I think so. Yes."

"You'll make something to take to them later today. To say thank you." She listened to him shift his weight, considering her punishment. "Borscht. Make a nice big pot for our lunch too. Plenty of cabbage, yes? We'll eat it together."

She stifled a belch, tasting bile.

"Whatever happened last night will not happen again." He moved toward the door. "I'll be home in two hours."

—⁂—

Even from the far end of the hallway, Ana could sense that something was wrong. The girls were clustered around a locker next to the science lab, and instinctively she knew that it was hers.

A few saw her approaching and whispered to the others. They'd been waiting for this moment. She was still ten, twelve steps away as the group scattered. Some went to their lockers; others brushed past her, maneuvering silent about-turns when they thought she wouldn't notice.

A couple of boys stood in her way, staring. She pushed by them, registering their faces reddening with glee and embarrassment.

The front of her locker door had been covered with tampons taped haphazardly around a giant pink card daubed with red letters.

CONGRATULATIONS ON BECOMING A WOMAN!

"What the hell?"

Ana heard Suvi's voice as if over a bad phone line. She allowed herself to be shoved out of the way, watching wordlessly as her friend tore down the card and screwed it into a ball.

Suvi turned on the cluster of girls, most of whom were now looking away. "Which one of you psycho bitches did this?" She snatched a handful of tampons and began cramming them into her bag.

"It's OK—"

"It is NOT OK, Ana." Suvi zipped her bag and flung it against the locker. "Where's Karen Spelberg?"

"She has math," someone said.

"I think I saw her in guidance."

"You're all liars and cowards and pathetic bully minions," hissed Suvi. "Come on, Ana."

She brushed roughly past Justin Cook, who had only just arrived, and muttered something under her breath. Ana watched Justin glance between them and the defaced locker and then laugh into the back of his hand. He didn't seem to recognize her from the party.

When they reached an empty stretch of corridor, Suvi stopped to drink from a water fountain.

"Thanks for that," said Ana.

"You don't have to thank me. But you should stand up for yourself more."

"They'd have wanted me to make a scene." Ana took a gulp of water. "It's not even true. I've had periods for two years."

"Karen Spelberg doesn't care. She's mean *and* dumb. She pulled that stunt on Josie Fu in grade seven. It was Josie's fault for being half Chinese and half Danish and therefore drop-dead gorgeous and therefore Karen's natural enemy." Suvi shouldered her bag. "No points for originality, but it still gets a reaction. People here have short memories."

Colony Felicidad

S ome short memories . . .

Picking stones with the little ones: Jonah and Benjamin Funk, Eva and Isaac Buhler, the twins Esther and Edith. Showing them how to sift through the dry soil and pick out the rocks and pebbles, just as Susanna had shown her years before, to clear the fields for planting. Hot work, sore backs, gritty nails, songs. Crickets trapped, trembling, on grass stalks. Afterward, lemonade under the *tipu* tree, whose roots grew thick and strong enough to upend a house.

Watching Agatha Bartsch sneak a look at Susanna's slate at school one morning. Catching Agatha's eye as she started to copy her answer. Feeling her humiliation, measuring it, before turning back to her own work. Agatha would not be coming back to school in the new year, anyway.

On Christmas Day, Agustín coming just before lunch with presents for the little ones: gourd rattles filled with rice. They chased each other around the table making a terrible noise until Susanna's mother shooed them all outside.

Her father, hunched over the dining table late at night with his paint tray and fine brushes. Sometimes he drew on cork, sometimes wood, cardboard when there was nothing else. Not pictures, but repeating patterns: diamonds and cubes and helixes and staircases that tricked the eye. Then he used a precision blade to cut the drawings into oddly shaped pieces. He gave some puzzles as gifts on birthdays. Mostly they stayed in a box on the dry sink.

Toronto

"WELL? ARE WE GOING to go in?"

The bus ride hadn't been as long as Ana had expected, and it had deposited them right outside the church. FIRST LIGHT MENNONITE CONGREGATION read the sign in arranged plastic letters. Easy.

She sensed Suvi growing impatient beside her. "Where are the wagons and braids and stuff? I wanted to see me some wagons and braids!"

"Oh, shush—I told you it's not like that here."

"Ana, do you want to find your mother or don't you?"

It had been Suvi's idea to come here. "It's called casing the joint," she'd told Ana. "If she's at the church often enough, we can get a look at her without being recognized ourselves. Before you have to meet her for real, you know?"

"She hasn't even responded to my questions yet."

"All the more reason to check up on her."

They tried the front door, but it was locked. "Let's see if there's another door by those bike racks," suggested Suvi.

There was—but it too was locked. There was a note on the door. *Hours: Monday–Friday, 8:30–6 p.m.* And below this, *Our Sunday services take place at the Danforth United Church. This location is open for day care and language classes only.*

Suvi groaned. "Dude. It didn't say this on the website?"

"I can't remember."

"I've got a tournament tomorrow—"

"My father will want me at church in the morning, anyway."

"You could ask him to try a new church?"

"He'd get suspicious. There isn't time this week . . ."

"Next week, then?"

"Maybe."

Miss G blinked at Ana, her small, wide-set eyes thoughtful behind her glasses. She looked like a kindly otter, thought Ana.

"There's no right answer," she said at last. "And you can always change your mind. The exercise is to get you thinking, that's all."

Ana stared at the four lines at the bottom of the page. Still blank, even after five minutes of Miss G trying to tease an answer out of her. At the top of the page were her answers to the multiple-choice questions they'd done in class that morning.

"Let's see . . . you like art. But you're also good at problem solving. You say you're very rational—I think I'd agree with that." Miss G scrolled down the page with her pencil. "What about managing an art gallery? That could be cool."

Ana nodded.

"Or teaching?"

Ana nodded again, but this time she looked away. She shouldn't be frustrated with Miss G. It wasn't her fault. In all her life until now, no one had ever asked Ana what she wanted to be. Back home, everyone just seemed to know what she would be: a daughter, a wife, a mother, a friend, a hard worker, a good Christian. How was she supposed to think of something to fill four lines about her desired career when everything she had counted on before—

"It's OK," said Miss G. "Let's leave this for now, and you can think about it."

Weird how you can be somewhere and the place you came from ceases to exist. Not really, but as good as. You *know* it's still there, that the people there are still going about their lives, washing clothes and milking cows, that the air still smells of soy and sorghum, that at night you'd still be able to hear the pigs snoring from the Reimers' barn—but really, you don't *believe* it. And the longer you're away, the harder you have to concentrate to summon up all of those things, to convince yourself that they're still really there: happening, breathing, being.

And you think for the longest time that you're going to miss it, and you do . . . but as the days and weeks pass, you miss it mainly because you're *used* to missing it. Missing it becomes something that you believe, rather than something that you actually do. After a little while, it's more work to think about missing it than it is to just get on with life. The new place is what's real, and the old place becomes a dream.

Colony Felicidad

"I don't mean to gossip, but . . ." Susanna drew the thread along her tongue before spearing it through the eye of the needle. "I saw Agatha Bartsch with Jacob Wolfe in the orchard yesterday."

"Together?"

A nod.

"They'd better be careful. Remember when her father found out about David stealing those oranges?"

Poor David. Agatha's father had walloped him with his own hand, and David had fled to hide in the forest for the rest of the day, not even coming in for dinner.

"I think they're serious."

"Justina says the Albertan kids used to call it *going steady.*"

"To hear her talk about it you'd think she'd gone to their high school."

"My grandmother called it a temple to sex, drugs and alcohol."

Susanna snorted. "She would."

We worked in silence for a while after that.

"Speaking of David . . ." Susanna steadfastly avoided looking at me, steering the inside-out shirt under the sewing machine. "Has he brought you any more gifts lately?"

A bright purple jay's feather; the dried-out shell of a wasp's nest; once, a yellow dorado he'd caught in the stream with Jacob Wolfe, still wet and glistening, its dead eyes bright.

"He'll have to ask my father first."

"Don't try and be coy. You're no good at it."

I looked at her. She was smiling. "As if your father would stop him. He's a teddy bear in wolf's clothing. And David's a good boy."

"That's the thing," I said. "I'm four months older than he is. I can remember when he still used to suck on his mother's apron strings." As if that wasn't bad enough, I towered a full head and shoulders over him too.

"Beggars can't be choosers, Anneli."

"*Excuse me.*"

"Well, you could do worse."

Toronto

ANA SPENT THAT SUNDAY in her room reading *Papillon*. She had considered doing as Suvi suggested and asking her father to take her to First Light that morning—but he had been in such a good mood, and she hadn't wanted to jeopardize it. They had made a few friends at the Baptist service, anyway; they would be missed if they didn't turn up this week without explanation.

The thin drizzle that grayed everything outside her window—people, cars, trees, sky—showed no sign of letting up. Ana didn't mind. She liked the way rainy days gave her permission to hide from the world. There was no expectation in a rainy day, no pressure to be outside enjoying something just because everyone else did.

Papillon wanted one thing: escape. So much so that he undertook such a series of wrongheaded, audacious, life-threatening risks, Ana couldn't believe that he'd ever live to tell the tale. But he had.

Strange, then, that when things finally seemed to be going his way—when he was living in secret with a village of pearl divers, happily married to a pair of sisters—he should decide that it was time to move on. And yet, if he hadn't, he wouldn't have been there to save some poor girl from shark-infested waters just a few chapters later.

Ana lingered over the pearl divers, the sisters with their twin babies by the same father, the girl struggling in the ocean. There she was—and there, and there. How could Mr. Peterson have known? Had he too felt this strange sensation when he read the book? Or was this the way with all books?

Escape: into another world, or into her own?

———

The school holiday concert was less a concert than a series of skits and a rowdy sing-along. There were Christmas lights on the stage and draped around the piano, and a musical performance by some of the teachers dressed as elves that made the kids in the audience burst into hoots and applause. But there were other parts that Ana had more difficulty understanding: the lighting of a menorah, which she found beautiful (the story was from the Old Testament; she would ask her father about it when she got home), and a dance set by a group of statuesque girls in saris, with kohl-rimmed eyes and little plastic jewels stuck to their foreheads.

"It's like Aladdin," she whispered to Suvi, who snorted and said, "Wrong country, dude."

Some of the older boys performed a rap about Kwanzaa while a slideshow behind them showed pictures of fruit and a candelabra like the menorah. They were boys that Ana used to be a little intimidated by. But now she found herself nodding to their beat, clapping along with everyone else for the final chorus.

———

Starting in November, she'd saved a dollar from each week's grocery budget for her father's Christmas present. Added to the collected small change from whatever was returned to her at the cash register, Ana had $9.74 by the last day of school.

She had survived the term. Earlier that week she had returned from the bathroom to geography to find that someone had written SKANK across the front of her agenda—on the other side of the classroom, Karen was winding her hair around a pencil and pursing her lips in a silent whistle—but there had been no more locker graffiti, and even Sean seemed to be running out of steam with the teasing. There had been whispers when Mr. Peterson asked Ana to stay behind after class one day—she had scored her first A on a test and he'd wanted to congratulate her—but Karen wasn't in her class and so the whispers had no fuel to flame into rumors.

Ana stopped in at Lenny's Hardware on the way home, leaving Suvi to fiddle with the gum machine at the front of the store. Down to the third aisle, past rows of X-Acto knives and precision instruments. A wood-handled awl cost $6.99 plus tax.

"You're the only person I know who gets her dad a knife for Christmas," said Suvi, popping a gumball into her mouth as they headed out.

"It's something he can use," said Ana. With the last of the money she'd got a musical card that played "Rudolph, the Red-Nosed Reindeer."

"Wanna go to the toboggan hill? It'll still be light for another half hour."

"I should stop at the library first. It'll be closed this weekend. My last chance until after Christmas."

Suvi's forehead crinkled. "Still hasn't written back, huh? Why don't we go back to that church once and for all and find out?"

"It's OK. It's a busy time of year." Ana pulled her toque down low over her eyes, trying to ignore the stinging in her nose. She had never felt coldness like this before. "For all I know, she could be on holiday."

—#—

Dear Ani,
I'm so sorry. No Internet at home and our office has been relocating, so I've been off-line for a while.

Ana frowned at the screen. Hadn't she heard of using the library?

You had some questions for me. I don't blame you! Kind of weird being asked, but of course you have every right. Here goes . . .
1. *The book must be the Shakespeare collection that was given to my parents on the way to Bolivia. Has your father really kept it all these years?*
2. *The curtains in your bedroom were plain blue, no pattern that I can remember.*

3. *My maiden name is Rempel, and my sister's middle name is Christina.*
4. *I think the watermelon incident happened when you were four and Maria told you that if you swallowed a watermelon seed, a watermelon would grow in your stomach. You were so upset you made yourself sick.*

Ana's pulse thudded in her temples. *And the gun in the lake?* she thought. But of course she hadn't asked about that. That would only scare her away. There would be plenty of time to ask the tricky questions.

I hope that convinces you. I'm happy to answer more questions if you think of any.
Maybe texting would be easier, though? Do you have a phone? We don't have to talk yet if you'd rather not. My number is 647-496-0921.
Love,
Mama
P.S. The pearls are yours.

⸻

"You press here for numbers, and here to go back to letters. Then, 'send.' And if you want to switch off predictive text, you go here . . . wait, let me find it . . ."

Ana craned her neck over Suvi's shoulder as she fiddled with the purple Nokia.

"OK, there. Your password is suvirox but you can change that if you want. The code's 1234 to top up your credit." Suvi handed her the cell. "I've put ten bucks on it already."

"You're amazing. I'll pay you back as soon as I can."

"No sweat. The phone only cost a few bucks. It's kind of a junky one, but it texts and makes calls. Call it my Christmas present to you. Now she can't fob you off with excuses about not having Internet, right?"

Ana hugged her.

"Whoa, jeez! Down, girl."

"Sorry, I'm just—"

"I know, it's cool. Hey, and it means I don't have to keep slipping notes through your letterbox. We can communicate like real people now."

"And Mischa's number is in here?"

"Yeah. Oh, and emergency calls are free. You know, like the fire department and police." Suvi slid off her bed and grabbed her bag. "Come on—we can test it out on the road."

—#—

Suvi: Merry Christmas, beeyatches! Hope you're having more fun than me. Julie's making us play charades and Steve is wasted on brandy and has acted out *Braveheart* like three times already. Ho! Ho! Ho!

Mischa: Merry Christmas, you guys. Mr. Winkler peed himself at lunch today just as Dad was bringing in the turkey. Not as bad as last year when EMS had to come for Mrs. Gage. Remember, S?

Suvi: Holy crap, yeah ☹ Ana, you OK?

Ana: Sorry—was at church. So different here. Everyone talks so much. Have to go. Stove lighter broken again.

Suvi: Dude, GET THEE A FREAKIN MICROWAVE!

Ana: Tell that to my father. More important: Lena texted back! Said maybe we could meet up in the new year.

Mischa: You going to?

Ana: ???!!!

Suvi: Best. Christmas. Present. EVER. Right?

Ana: ☺

Every year, Suvi's parents threw an early New Year's party for their neighbors up and down the street.

"It's become kind of a tradition," Suvi told Ana when they met up at the toboggan hill on Boxing Day. "The people on either side of us always come, and the Richardsons, and Mrs. Patel and her daughter, and the Greek family with all those kids, and Jonty and Ben and their folks, and Mr. de Wet brings that *biltong* stuff that he dries himself, and there are always loads of randoms whose names I can never remember. Steve makes a huge goulash and people bring cookies and butter tarts and stuff and we basically pretend it's New Year's Eve but everyone gets to go home at, like, eleven so it's not as exhausting for the little kids. Mischa's going to be away with his folks, but you and your dad should totally come."

Ana took this all in, watching half a dozen snowsuited boys attempt to steer a chain of flying saucers down the hill. As the chain gathered speed, it doubled over on itself and two of the boys went flying into the slush. Their eyes shone black and bright beneath their woolly hats, and their teeth in their laughing mouths gleamed white. The flush in their cheeks was the only color in a field of gray.

"I'll mention it to him," Ana said.

"Mr. Rempel—we meet at last!"

An explosion of laughter burst from the living room, where music was playing, as Julie took their coats. Women in lipstick and glittery dresses filled the hallway with a bright, perfumed haze; the men, more casually dressed, walked around in stocking feet. Some children crowded down the hallway on their way upstairs, and Ana was aware of yet more guests arriving up the front path behind them. "You guys are on coat duty until everyone's here, OK?" Julie told her. "Suvi will show you where we've made space for them in the rec room downstairs." She turned back to Ana's father, who was taking it all in with an expression of bewildered amusement. "Mr. Rempel—I'm so sorry. I'm Julie. And I think you've met Steve outside the house before?"

"Please, call me Miloh."

"Miloh!" Julie grinned broadly, and took him by the shoulders. "Come on in to the kitchen before Steve kicks everyone out—when he's cooking he turns into a real tyrant. There's mulled wine, or beer if you prefer . . ."

Ana watched them go as she followed Suvi down the narrow basement stairs. "Do your parents know he doesn't drink?" she whispered.

"I think I mentioned it," said Suvi. "But there's Coke and stuff too. Relax, Ana—he'll be fine."

—#—

The goulash was late, and one of the neighbors had to run back across the street to get more dressing when it turned out that Julie hadn't made enough for both salads, but nobody minded. They stuck another log on the fire, and Ana's father managed to tease the dwindling flames back to a mighty roar, which made everyone in the living room applaud and cheer as if he'd just scored the winning goal at the Stanley Cup. Ana was the only one who noticed the color rise to his cheeks, saw in his smile a modest thrill. He caught her eye and raised his eyebrows as if to say, *These people are crazy, but who am I to complain?*

So she was happy and confident, by the time she found herself lining up for food, that he could fend perfectly well for himself in this strange world of skimpy dresses and loud music and wine stains on one arm of the couch. At one point she had heard him talking to some other men about the porch that he'd rebuilt for Mrs. Fratelli; later, one of the neighbors asked if he wanted to help flood the neighborhood ice rink later that week, when it would be cold enough for the kids to start skating outside again. Ana's father had grinned and nodded, and reached across the table for another Orangina.

She was sitting in the kitchen, waiting for Suvi to join her, when she became aware of a chair scraping next to her. It was Jonty, the boy from three doors down, wearing a velvet blazer, balancing a plate overfilled with goulash and bread rolls and a dollop of taramasalata from the buffet table.

"Hi," he said. "Ana, right?"

Ana nodded. "And . . . Jonty?"

"John. Jonathan."

Ana nodded. She remembered him from the summer, when he'd seemed to consider her with distaste and vague disappointment. She studied him now as he ate and decided that it was actually a look of concentration, a look that suggested that he found it easier to *think* about people than talk to them.

"Is that wine?" she asked.

"Shiraz," he said. "Would you like some? My dad brought it."

"No, thanks."

"Hey, Jonty. Budge over." Suvi nudged her plate onto the bar stool next to him. "Jeez, is that a smoking jacket?"

"Do you like it?"

"Did it come with a pipe?" Suvi jabbed at some goulash with her fork, sending a piece of onion splattering across the floor. "Aw, crap."

"Nice one, Fidgety Philip," remarked Jonty.

"Very funny. Hold on, I'm going to get some paper towel."

When she'd gone, Ana looked at Jonty. "Fidgety Philip?" she said. "Zappel-Philipp?"

He smiled. "You know Struwwelpeter?"

"Do people read that here?"

"Not generally. But I'm into old German stuff."

Ana nodded. It was hard to tell from the way he spoke whether he was being sarcastic or deadly earnest. Perhaps this was something all the boys learned at his school. Then again, perhaps it was just Jonty.

John. Jonathan.

"The music in there is getting out of control. Every year, Suvi's parents get a little more trendy."

Ana strained her ears over the chatter and clatter of dishes.

"I don't know this song."

"It's hipster stuff."

Ana shrugged. "I kind of like it."

"So, Plattdeutsch?"

"Yes. Only, if you were talking about Mennonites, you'd say Plautdietsch. It's like regular Low German with a special accent."

"It sounds strange. Almost, I don't know . . . Dutch, or something."

Ana nodded. Suvi still hadn't returned—one of Steve's work friends had trapped her in the hallway to ask about babysitting rates—and in a way Ana was glad. John's plate had been empty for at least the last ten minutes. If he'd wanted to escape their conversation about declensions and vowel lowering, he would have had the perfect excuse.

Instead, he asked, "What do you think of Walpole?"

"It's OK. Different."

"Not kind of feral?"

" . . . ?"

"You know, wild? Hairy?"

"Oh, yes. The kids there are not very disciplined." Ana inclined her head toward the living room. "My father would say."

"My father would agree. My mother thinks it's the real world. If it were up to her, that's where we'd go to school."

"The real world is wherever you are, I think. Not one or the other."

Jonty nodded. "Fair point," he said.

"John, we're going!" Ben poked his head around the kitchen door. "Dad says can you get our coats? Mom and Julie are doing their long good-bye thing."

"As usual." Jonty drained his glass and set it on the table.

"I can show you where to find the coats," said Ana. "You didn't get here that early, so they should be near the top of the heap."

"Lay on, Macduff."

They passed Suvi in the dining room, where she was being grilled on school matters by old Mrs. Patel. Suvi grimaced at Ana, who gestured to the basement steps. "Just one minute," she mouthed.

Ana went sideways down the narrow staircase, partly to avoid slipping and partly because it felt strange to be walking with Jonty behind her; she felt a need to face him as they talked.

"There was a system to begin with," she said. "Then some of the little kids tried to help and it got a bit messed up. The rule was supposed to be that only Suvi and I would come down here, so we'd be able to keep track of everyone's stuff . . ."

"Jesus. A coat-check cartel."

"What do your coats look like?"

Jonty glanced through the pile. "I don't see them here. Ben's is bright yellow. As in, stupid bright. Visible-from-space bright."

"They must be in the back, then."

She led him through the rec room and into the empty workout room that Steve's rowing machine shared with the boiler. She reached around the door to flip on the light switch, but stopped as she felt him take her hand.

Ana turned and found Jonty standing suddenly quite close. He was watching her with a serious expression, as if waiting to decide something—or waiting for her to decide.

"John! Dad says hurry up!" bellowed Ben from the top of the stairs.

He leaned in abruptly, tightening his hold on her hand for just a second. His lips tasted of wine; he breathed softly through his nose, warm on her cheek.

"John!" Heavy footsteps on the stairs.

"Dammit . . ." He pulled away, letting go of her hand. "There they are—the yellow one and the red one and the two black ones. Here, I've got it . . ."

She watched as he bundled them under both arms. "Happy New Year," she said, just as Ben arrived to take his coat from his brother.

Jonty smiled quickly—a light turned on and off again. "Thanks," he said. "And to you too, *Mejal*."

—

"Well," her father said, as they crossed the street back to their house. "That really was quite a lovely evening."

Ana didn't think she'd ever heard her father use the word "lovely" before. She felt her breath swing back toward her through the frosty darkness and was glad when a car rumbled by behind them, drowning out the sound of her still thumping heart.

—

She didn't tell Suvi about what had happened with Jonty. Suvi would have squealed and demanded details, or else she would have pulled a face and teased Ana about it for weeks. Either way, Ana would have had to try to explain something she herself didn't understand.

—

Later, it would occur to Ana that her first visit to the beach should have been in the summer. Sand sticking to sunscreen, the smack and bounce of a beach ball skimming a net, children squealing as they flirted with the surf.

But it was mid-January as she sat on the Queen East streetcar, staring through the grubby condensation at slush-tracked side streets and the desolate snow-covered beach. Every surface that wasn't covered with snow was crusted with salt, and she found herself thinking of the salt fields in Bolivia: great expanses of dazzling white that made you thirsty just to look at them, and traces from dried-up volcanoes that left cracked hexagons in the surface, like the patterns her father etched into cork and cardboard.

Lena had suggested that they meet at the Goof—"Get off at Beech, cross the street and it's the Chinese restaurant with a 1950s sign outside," her text said, and Ana spotted it almost as soon as she stepped off the streetcar. The neon sign spelled out "Good" in vertical letters and "Food" in horizontal ones; above this, "Garden Gate" was spelled out in loopy cursive. Enormous diner windows made it easy to see in. A family was being served steaming plates of chow mein at a central table while an older man sat on a bar stool, reading a newspaper and absently tapping his coffee mug with one finger.

She's not here.

Ana forced herself to go in, slipping into a booth near the door so that she could watch people as they entered.

She's not coming.

The plastic tabletops had been made to look like wood. A laminated menu listed lunch specials on one side, drinks and desserts on the other. Ana stared at it, pretending to ponder her order. She looked around for the toilets. If she had to throw up, she'd probably have five seconds, tops, to get inside—

"You look like a lime juice kind of girl," said a voice next to her. An elderly waitress licked her thumb and flipped to a fresh page in her notebook. "Or a hot chocolate, given how cold it is today. You ready to order?"

"I'm waiting for someone," said Ana.

"No problem. I'll bring some water in the meantime."

———

What was "a lime juice kind of girl" supposed to look like?

Fresh panic. Was she being watched even now, by a woman sitting in a car across the road? Sizing her up? "A lime juice kind of girl." Sour? Green? Chilly?

There was no car; there was no woman. But Ana imagined herself peering through the misted diner window at the girl hunched alone in a corner booth, nose stung red by the cold, awkward in her own skin, dwarfed by her parka. She had taken off her hat but not her scarf; pools of brown water were forming under her salt-stained boots. Is that the daughter Lena would choose to bring back into her life, given the chance?

Of course she's not coming.

———#———

"They do an all-day breakfast too, you know. The banana pancakes are kind of amazing."

Ana looked up, ready to deflect another waitress. But the woman standing in front of her wore a long patchwork coat and slouchy, snow-dusted boots. Her hair shimmered with tiny frozen droplets and her cheeks were flushed from the cold.

"Can I . . . ?" The woman put her arms out, made as if to hug her—then froze. Ana had stood up, flinched at the sudden gesture like a startled animal. "Sorry, I didn't mean to—"

"It's fine," said Ana, watching her sit down and wishing, *wishing*, that she hadn't jumped like that.

She backed into the booth. "I might just get a coffee."

"Sure. You're not too young for that? I mean, you like coffee? But sure, totally. Totally. Where's Meg?" The woman began to take off her coat, catching the waitress's eye. She mimed two coffees. "And a slice of coconut cream pie. Two forks."

It didn't feel strange, exactly. It didn't feel of anything. If Ana had passed this woman on the street, she wouldn't have given her a second thought.

"Wow. You're gorgeous, do you know that? Like how I imagined, only . . ." She shook her head, wiped her eyes. "Taller. *So* tall, like your father. Like a goddess. My beautiful daughter . . ."

The middle part of her mother's face was familiar, but the flesh around it had filled out, obscuring those bits Ana should have recognized. An attractive face, not as young as she'd expected. More surprising was the way she wore her hair like a mane down her back, dangly gold earrings with little colored glass beads, a scarf unwound to reveal layered V-necks. There was nothing of Colony Felicidad here, no trace of those people, that life.

They sat, facing one another.

"First thing's first. You know it's not really smart to meet with people you've only ever talked to online, right? Does your dad know you're here?"

"No."

"Does anyone?"

"No."

"Can I give you a piece of advice, then? This is a bad idea. Don't do this kind of thing again, OK?"

Don't meet my mother who left when I was five again?

"And try some of the pie. You'll thank me."

They waited in silence as the waitress put out the coffee, plates and forks. When she had turned away, Ana said, "Lena."

Her mother looked up.

"Is that what you're called now?"

Her mother nodded. "Yes. And . . . Ana?"

"It was his idea. I like it, though."

"That's OK, then."

It was about as awkward as having a conversation with a nice enough stranger, but no worse. Ana waited until her mother looked down to spear a piece of pie before studying her face, searching for some sign of herself. She did not want to be caught staring. The nose that wasn't her father's: was it like this woman's, straight and square at the tip? The voice, sweetly husky: Ana had always thought her own was low, glottal, un-feminine. Aspects of herself that she had always wondered about—her appearance, her personality—could have been a part of this woman too. Or not. Where did they connect?

"How is he? Your father."

"He's fine. He's looking for you."

Her mother breathed deeply. "You've been here how long?"

"About ten minutes."

"No . . . I mean, in the city?"

"Oh. Uh, a few months."

"Why, though? Why would he do this?"

"I don't know—he won't tell me. There were some things . . ." Ana looked out the window. "He argued with Gerhard Buhler just before we left."

Lena said something under her breath. Then, "Are you in school?"

"Yeah."

"Is it hard?"

"Math is really hard. English and history are OK because I have a scribe to help with writing in English. Art is good. The teacher lets us listen to music while we paint. I'm learning French too." She stirred her coffee.

"And what about the other students? Made any friends?"

"A couple."

"Cool kids?"

"Cool-nice? Or Cool-*cool*?"

"You tell me."

"Suvi doesn't have a clique. I guess she's too cool for one. But she wouldn't call herself cool, you know?"

"Totally. She sounds great."

That voice: prodding, weighing, colluding, approving. Was that the voice she'd carried in her head all these years? The what-would-Mama-say voice? Was that the same as a conscience or a memory? Or just one of the voices that crazy people were said to hear?

"Why Toronto? Why didn't you go back to Alberta?" Ana asked.

"I didn't have anyone left there. Everyone had gone south years ago."

"Why not Aylmer, then? Where Johan and Katherina live?"

"How do you know about them?"

"We went to see them. Papa knew you wouldn't be there, but I think he hoped they would know how to find you."

Lena nodded. "You know, I've never met them. I knew that I had cousins in Ontario, which was better than nothing. But in the meantime, here I found a church, a community . . ."

"First Light."

"Yeah, really close by. It's kind of different from what I guess you're used to. It's more . . . relaxed. And diverse. Lots of immigrants go there. I volunteer to help them with their English. You should come with me some time."

"Sure." Ana stirred her drink. "How did you do it? Practically, I mean. How did you get all this way? Flights are expensive."

"I worked as a cleaner in La Paz for a few months. Saved up enough to bribe a guy at the consulate to get me on a flight. He signed something saying I had a family emergency. Which, in a sense, it was." Ana didn't return her smile. "Look, Ani . . ." The woman across from her suddenly became a stranger again. She reached for Ana's hand, then appeared to think better of it. "I don't know what to say. I'm sorry. I'm sorry for . . . There are things I couldn't control. I can't apologize for things that weren't my fault. That you can't understand."

"Try me."

"Excuse me?" A grunt of disbelief. "Is this how the kids talk in Colony Felicidad now?"

"We're not in Colony Felicidad."

Her mother nodded, took a mouthful of coffee. "Fair enough. OK."

How did she compare to the women Ana had observed when they first arrived in the city, wondering who among them belonged to her? Probably, if Ana had seen Lena at a bus stop, or in the grocery store, she would have picked her as a promising prospect. Not beaten down, not a shadow, not a weirdo. Not a mother in mourning, either.

Was she disappointed?

"Do you remember that day at the lake?" Ana asked. "When you saved Isaac Buhler from drowning?"

—⁎—

Lena paid for everything, of course. Because she was the adult, and because Ana had no change, only bus tokens. Eventually Ana found the words to ask where the money came from.

"Do you work now?"

"Monday to Thursday. In a law firm."

Ana frowned.

"I know, right?" said Lena. "And the crazy thing is, it's not just as a cleaner or something like that. I'm a legal *secretary*."

"What's that?"

"Like a secretary, but more specialized. It means I know words like *habeas corpus* and *actus reus*." She pulled her hair back into a ponytail, rolled an elastic from her wrist. "One of the women who volunteer in the English program at church is married to a lawyer. He let me come in to do some filing a few hours a week. Then he suggested I think about training. It's a small firm, but they sponsored me to do a community college course. One year in total, and I kept up the filing work in the meantime to buy food. Shared a room with another girl from church. I've had this job and my own place for, what . . . almost eight years now. Crazy!"

"Yeah. Wow." Ana bit off a piece of skin peeling from her fingernail. "Maybe I could see your office some time."

Lena's face fell—only for an instant, as she looked away—but then she returned Ana's look with a smile.

"Maybe," she said.

"Do they know about me?"

"They're really nice people." Lena rewound her scarf around her neck. "They don't ask a lot of questions."

She made it home before her father, with time to spare, and the first thing she did was to set the water boiling for lunch. Food first, always. The hallmark of a normal, functioning household.

When he came in, he turned the lock behind him before dropping the spare quarters in the tray by the front door. It was now a daily ritual. Ana judged by the clink of change that he may not even have made a phone call that morning.

"I'm in the kitchen," she called. Testing her voice before she'd have to look him in the eye.

He came in and sat down at the table, running a hand through his hair.

"Did you have a good morning?" she asked.

"I sat in the Baptist church," he said flatly. "It's very peaceful in there when no one's playing a guitar."

"I can imagine."

"And you? You saw Suvi?"

"No, I stayed in." Ana leaned into the steam, allowing it to moisten her cheeks. He mustn't catch her blushing; he could read a lie a mile off. "I had a lot of schoolwork."

"I don't understand the schools here. You do more work at home than you do with the teacher. You could read when you were seven. How much else can there be to learn?"

There was no point trying to explain things like history and geography and French and biology and chemistry to him, even less so world religions or social studies or gym. Ana stirred the rice and turned the quick-cook casserole out of its paper tray, then set the plates on the table.

"Please don't say anything to him," Lena had begged when they parted. "I'm not ready. I need to decide how to deal with this."

Apparently she had heard the receptionist at church asking one of the older members if they knew of a Helena and discovered that a message had been left on the notice board seeking a possible member of the congregation. But that had been during the summer, and there had been no follow-up. She had chalked it up to coincidence and banished it from her mind. "If I'd expected to hear from him, perhaps I would have paid more attention," she said.

Ana sat down opposite her father and nudged at her food with her fork while he ate hungrily. When he had finished, he brought his workbox down from a cabinet and laid out his latest project on the table. It was a double-sided puzzle. On one side was carved an image of their house in Colony Felicidad, the walls and roof and sky patterned with an intricate web of repeating shapes. On the other side was a simplified version of the subway map he'd studied at the bus stop down the street. Ana's father had yet to travel on the subway, but the idea of it fascinated him.

"You should do blocks next," she said. "Six sides. Six puzzles."

Her father only grunted.

"Two is enough for now," he said.

—#—

Lena had said she wanted to take Ana shopping, so they met the following Saturday outside a neon blue shop front in Kensington Market.

"We can go in there if you want," she said. "It's secondhand stuff, but vintage, which means it'll be stylish. If you don't mind searching a bit, there are some good finds."

They quickly settled on a stack of jingling beaded bracelets and a silk scarf that Lena tied artfully around Ana's neck. "Accent pieces," she said. "Now we find a silhouette."

The silhouette turned out to be a thin gray turtleneck and black wool miniskirt. "Short on the bottom, covered up on top," said Lena. "Or vice versa. That's how you avoid looking cheap. Next, shoes . . ."

She had hardly stopped speaking since she'd arrived, coffee in hand, flustered and apologetic for being late.

"You don't need height, but ankle boots would be cute. Look at these."

Black suede boots with tassels and a gold heel were added to the stash, followed by a pair of pink moccasins at the cash register "because they're totally impractical and I saw you stop to look at them twice."

"Suvi will either love them or think they're crazy," said Ana.

"Sounds like win-win to me. I'm starving—what about you?"

They turned onto a little street lined with Chinese restaurants, variety stores and Internet cafés. Every awning, sign and menu was covered in Chinese, apart from the Visa and Mastercard stickers taped to the windows. Lena steered her into a café where Ana collapsed into a chair, glad to escape the noise and swirl of the street. A minute later, her mother returned with two glasses filled with ice cubes swirling in cream. "Honey milk tea," she said, "with tapioca bubbles."

It was almost sickeningly sweet, the jelly pearls slimy and slick in her throat.

"How do you know about all this?" Ana asked, as Lena returned from the counter for a second time, sliding a plate of dumplings onto the table before snapping apart two chopsticks and jabbing one into a soft, sauce-speckled belly.

"When I moved here, I found it too depressing trying to cook the old stuff on my own," she said between mouthfuls. "So I ate out where it was cheap, and where there was life." She nudged a dumpling toward Ana. "Let me guess: this is your first time eating Chinese food."

Ana looked directly at her mother. She could tell that Lena wanted it to be true, that she was eager to be the one to have given her this first experience, to have opened Ana's eyes to a new and exciting thing.

"Actually, no," she said. "This guy at school got me dim sum once."

Lena blinked. Did she look wounded, or just surprised? But she recovered quickly, found a way once more to be the older, wiser one. "Oh?" she said, eyebrows rising. "A guy? Tell me."

"Just a guy. His name's Tom."

"I see."

Ana felt her cheeks turn hot, took another gulp of the bubble tea in a bid to cool down.

"It wasn't a date. He's a teacher. We're just friends."

A mistake. Lena set the chopsticks on her plate and stiffened.

"You went out for a meal with your teacher? With other kids?"

"No, just us."

"What was he doing taking a fourteen-year-old girl out? You call him Tom?"

"Obviously not. But it's none of your business." Ana set her glass down. "Can I have some water, please?"

"Don't talk to me like that, Ani."

"Then don't get on your high horse about some stupid dim sum. It's not like he's going to abduct me." *Purple ribbons tied to lampposts, trees, iron railings—is that what Lena thought would happen?* "It's not a problem. And even if it was, it's not *your* problem."

"I'm your *mother*."

"As far as he's concerned, you're dead." *Too far. Take it back.* "Never mind, OK?"

"What do you mean, dead?"

Ana rolled her eyes. "It's easier to say that here. If I say my parents are divorced, people will think it's weird that I live with my dad. You'd have to have done something really bad . . ."

Silence. They hadn't talked once about Papa yet. Or about Colony Felicidad, or anything to do with the last ten years.

"Can I have some water, please?" Ana said.

"Sure. I'll get you a glass with the bill."

———#———

Farther down the street, they passed a young man taking photos of people with a Polaroid camera. There was a backdrop for posing against—on one side a Parisian music hall, the other a beach— and a box of props: boas, floppy hats, plastic martini glasses, a cigarette holder, an umbrella, a beach ball. The sign on the sidewalk said $2 A PHOTO.

"Uh-uh," said Ana, noticing Lena pause over the sign. "No way."

"It'll take two seconds," said Lena. "It'll be fun. And I want a photo with you."

"You can take one with your phone."

"The camera's no good on my phone. Besides, I want something that will last." She was already rummaging in her purse for the change. "Here," she said, flagging the young man down. "Which one should we have, Ani, the music hall or the beach?"

"I really don't care."

"The beach, then. We can pretend it's summer, right?"

The young man fiddled idly with his camera while Lena bent over the props box. She handed Ana the beach ball and a sun hat and wound a boa around her own shoulders. "I'll spin the parasol like this, and you throw the ball up on the count of three, OK?" she said.

"Are you ready?" asked the young man.

"Never been readier," said Lena. "OK, Ana? One, two . . . three!"

———⁂———

Lena loved it. She kept saying so, all the way back to the streetcar.

"It's surreal," she said. "Like something Man Ray would have done."

"Who?"

"I love that you're not even looking at the camera, you're watching the ball. Deadpan. The way you threw it straight up in the air, it's like a Japanese lantern or a beach ball of Damocles hanging over you. And do I look committable, or what?"

"It's pretty weird."

"It IS pretty weird. We're pretty weird. Look, is that your streetcar?"

"I think so."

"I don't want your father to start worrying. Catch this one now and we'll sort out plans for next week by text, OK? Maybe we can catch an exhibition."

"Sure. Thanks for all this stuff. And for lunch."

"We had a great time. I had a great time, anyway—I hope you did. Here, keep this." She slipped the photo into Ana's bag, shaking her head as Ana began to protest. "No, I mean it. It's yours."

Only later did Ana find herself thinking that perhaps Lena had wanted her to want the photo, all along.

"Where did you get those clothes?" her father asked over dinner that night.

"Suvi," replied Ana. *How stupid to have forgotten to take them off. Sometimes, Ana—*

"Tell her she can have the skirt back. And you don't wear that jewelry outside of the house."

"Look at me—I'm Amy Winehouse!" Karen Spelberg leaned across the lab table, holding the beaker filled with baking soda over the Bunsen burner flame. She pressed a finger to one nostril and pretended to inhale the white powder.

"Moron. You smoke that stuff. And you look more like Peaches Geldof anyway," said one of her friends.

"I thought that was heroin?"

"Urgh! You guys. OK, Whitney Houston. *And I-eee-yaiiii . . . will always love yooooouuu . . .*"

"Philip Seymour Hoffman," said Suvi under her breath. "You've got his figure."

"I don't understand," said Ana in a low voice, pushing the calculator across the table to Suvi.

"No, I got the same answer. If we add 3.5 mg, then it will be—"

"I mean Karen."

"She's pretending to be a crackhead."

"You mean crazy?"

"Jeez, Ana, did you grow up in a cave? Crack, you know? Cocaine? The drug? You, like, heat it up and smoke it. Or snort it." Suvi checked the numbers against her worksheet, started erasing a few. "It's what desperate junkies do, and super-rich celebrities. Doesn't really matter. It messes you up, either way. If it doesn't kill you." She blew off the eraser grit, corrected the numbers. "It's basically really, really stupid—kind of like someone else we know."

Ana bit her lip. Karen was now tearing off strips of her worksheet and fluttering them over the open flame, hand cupped over her mouth to control her laughter. Suvi rolled her eyes.

"She's going to have to stay in over lunch to finish her lab. She won't think it's so funny, then."

—#—

How about a movie ? The Swimmer on at the Lihgtbox, Saturday 2pm. We can let Burt Lancaster do the talking.

Ana must have read the text a hundred times, memorized the mixed-up letters in "Lightbox" and the extra space after "movie" until they appeared not as errors but inevitabilities. The message was so . . . *casual.* Two months ago, if someone had told Ana she'd be receiving messages like this from her mother, she would have laughed in disbelief.

Wasn't this what she'd wanted all along? Wasn't this better than anything she'd dared to hope for? Then why did it make her feel as if she was clinging to a runaway train?

She didn't reply for two days.

```
Sounds fun but can't. Big math test on Monday—sorry.
```

Within fifteen minutes, a reply:

Understand. Next week?

Ana deleted it and switched off her phone.

Did you get my last msg? Wanted to know if nxt week good for u.

I think so. Maybe Sunday afternoon.

Great ☺ Lightbox at 2?

OK

—#—

Sorry, can't do Sunday after all. School thing.
Sorry again. Will txt soon.

—#—

Ani, just say if you don't want to meet up. L

I do, just been really busy.

*Only if you're sure. We could go see the Incas at the museum
anytime. Your call.*

—#—

How's Thursday? I get off school at 3.

—#—

"Wait a minute . . . your dad doesn't know?"

Second lunch, an empty classroom. They sat on the high window
ledge by the heater, feet propped on the back of two chairs. Candy
wrappers littered the floor; on one of the desks, a half-eaten sandwich

slumped next to a forgotten thermos decorated with anarchy As. Suvi pushed her sweatshirt hood off her head. *"Still?"*

"I've only met her twice. The first time was too soon, and she asked me not to say anything."

"You spent a whole day with her at Kensington Market. He must know something's up."

"I told him I was with you."

"Dude, that's not always going to work." Suvi gulped down her Coke. "He's looking for her too, remember. What if he finds her? Are you going to pretend you've never met?"

Ana shrugged.

"OK, it's not for me to say. This whole thing is crazy." Suvi pulled her sleeves over her hands. "I wish this school would invest in some decent heating."

"Do you want my gloves?"

"Ana, Hello Kitty is for six-year-olds and hot, ironic-cool Japanese girls. I hate to break it to you, but you are neither. Next time Lena takes you shopping, get her to buy you some normal gloves, OK?"

"OK."

"Let me see the picture again." Ana unzipped the outer pocket of her bag and handed her the Polaroid. "She looks really young, doesn't she?"

"She's thirty-four."

"How'd she get to be so cool?" Suvi's nose crinkled. "I mean, no offense, but compared to you . . ."

"She's lived here for a decade. Her church is much more liberal. She has a smartphone and she goes to movies. And she was born here too. Bolivia was never really her home."

"You don't seem that excited, Ana. This is a big deal!"

"I am excited. But not in the way I thought I would be. She's just a person, you know? Not perfect. Not awful. She's really nice. But . . . it's as though something's missing."

"She's keeping her guard up too?"

"Maybe. Maybe she's scared of frightening me off." Ana frowned.

"But then she says things like 'I'm your *mother*' . . . and she hasn't even been around for the last ten years . . ."

"She's figuring it out too," said Suvi. "How to be a mother, I mean. Like you're figuring out how to be a daughter." Suvi started to crush her Coke can.

"I suppose." Next to Ana was a pile of worksheets left behind by a previous class. Word searches, probably brought in by a substitute teacher. Ana reached for the pile and arranged them in order of completeness. *Firecracker, spaceship, mountain, mystery.*

"Hey, you could try to re-introduce them! Like, as if it were an accident, only not. In an Italian restaurant. Have you seen *The Parent Trap*?" Suvi tapped the can against her knee. "Of course you haven't. But it could totally work."

"I don't know."

"You're seeing her when? Do you think I could tag along? Follow you at a distance?"

"No way. It's weird enough as it is."

"Fine." Screwed-up chip packets skittered across one of the desks as the door opened and a grade ten class began to filter in. "But text me when you have a second, OK? I want details."

---***---

Capacocha was the Inca term for human sacrifice. Ceremonies were conducted at times of crisis or mourning and involved children between the ages of six and fifteen. Young victims were favored as they were valued for their spiritual purity and physical health. In recent years, archaeologists have discovered several burial sites in the Andean mountains where the victims' bodies have been almost perfectly preserved thanks to the extreme cold and dry air.

The bracelets could have hung on a display in any one of the stores in Kensington Market: aquamarine beads laced onto a black leather thong, chevron earrings dangling with cowry shells. Ana pressed her nose to the glass, imagining their cool weight against her skin.

In preparation for the pilgrimage that would preface a sacrifice, the children were fattened on a diet rich in maize and meat. Then they would be presented to the emperor in Cuzco dressed in elaborate costumes and fine jewelry. Over a hundred such ornaments were found with the children at one burial site, of which several are displayed here.

Ana peered at the photograph of the dead girl's body. Her legs were crossed, torso doubled over so that her hair, still braided, fell across her leathered face.

Sacrifices took place on high mountaintops where the thin air could be difficult to breathe. For this reason, the victims were fed coca leaves on the climb to ensure that they reached the ceremonial site alive. A sedative drink was delivered to minimize pain and panic before the victim was strangled or killed with a blow to the head.

Ana pulled away from the display and looked around for her mother. There she was, across the room, studying a string fringed with dozens of knotted cords, like a mop spread flat. Ana turned back to the display of the girl, the jewelry and the pile of dried green leaves.

The coca plant was believed to have magical properties and was frequently used in religious ceremonies, as well as for healing purposes and as an anesthetic. It remains popular to this day, both chewed raw and as the basis for the refined powder that makes cocaine.

Colony Felicidad

W e weren't supposed to know about the King of Cocaine. Only Susanna and I knew, and Maria, who told us because Agustín had told her. The King's real name was Roberto Suárez Goméz. His ancestors had been rubber barons who enslaved and brutalized the Caripuña people on the Madeira River a hundred years earlier, during the rubber boom. Nowadays, rubber was old hat. Nowadays, if you wanted to get rich, it was all about cocaine.

Peasants had grown coca for thousands of years, mainly for chewing. Then in the 1970s, a powder made from coca leaves became a fashionable drug all around the world. Suárez bought the airplanes and built the airstrips necessary to export cocaine from Bolivia to Paraguay and beyond, and in doing so he became super rich. Because he had family members in high positions in Bolivia's fascist military government, he not only was never persecuted for growing a massive illegal drug trade, he received military protection too. Although he made no secret of living the high life, he also gave a lot of money to charity: developing the poorest regions in the country, building hospitals, introducing safe drinking water and electricity to isolated communities, that sort of thing. The coca producers who worked for him became a part of La Corporación; the way they saw it, they weren't being exploited in the least. Suárez even offered to pay off all of Bolivia's foreign debt—at the time, about $3 billion—if the Americans would drop trafficking charges against him. (They didn't.)

In the end, of course, things didn't work out so well for him. The government changed, and he was jailed in 1988 for eight years. I think he died not long after that. But the craze for cocaine that he'd helped to feed just kept getting bigger and bigger.

According to Agustín, tourists who came to Bolivia for backpacking holidays often paid up to 150 Bolivianos for a single gram of cocaine. That's about $20, which seems like quite a lot for a quarter of a teaspoon of something, no matter what it is.

Toronto

"DID YOU EVER GO to Moth?"

Lena had been reading the note about the *quipa*, but now she straightened, turning with a quizzical look to Ana.

"Moth? I never went, no. Why do you ask?"

"There was a bus that used to go that way. I just always wondered about it."

"*Moth*." Lena turned the word over in her mouth. "I'm pretty sure your father made a trip there, way back when. Maybe a couple of times when you were a baby." She switched her bag onto her other shoulder as they made their way into the next room.

"Why'd he go there?"

"Business, I guess. Not something I asked about." They had reached a display map of Peru. "Now there's somewhere I'd like to visit. Wouldn't that be something? The Inca Trail? How much do you think it would cost?"

Ana shook her head.

"Anything's possible," said Lena, moving away from the map. "Maybe one day we'll go."

———— # ————

"Did you ever get the postcards I sent you?" Lena's fork hovered over her salad. The sounds of clattering dishes and chatter resonated through the cafeteria, a contrast to the hush of the gallery rooms upstairs. "The ones with old-fashioned book covers on them? *The Snow Queen? Peter and Wendy?* There were others too . . ."

Ana forced herself to swallow her mouthful of tuna sandwich. She nodded.

"Yeah," she said. *"King Arthur."*

Lena's face lit up. "That's right! Oh, I'm glad. I was afraid your father . . ."

Ana let her mother's sentence peter out. She did not have the stomach to explain that Papa had never said the postcards came from Toronto. He'd never said where they came from, period. The books they depicted were not the sorts of books that were read in Colony Felicidad. Ana was allowed to look at them by special request; the rest of the time, they stayed locked on the top shelf of the dry sink.

"For every postcard I sent you, I bought the actual book for myself. I liked to look at their spines all lined up and think of you looking at the postcards in your room."

It had never occurred to Ana to feel sorry for her mother. Now, for the first time, something in Lena's voice touched her.

"I liked the one about King Arthur," Ana said. "With the sunset."

"Oh, yes, that's a good one. Funny, I always thought of it as the sun rising." Lena picked through the remaining salad leaves, the tough stems and tickling curls that were hard to chew. "On nights when I can't sleep, when I end up watching the sunrise, it makes me feel hopeful in the same way. Because it's not a sad picture, is it? There's too much light. Sad is the hours before the light—the blue hours."

When she was younger, and thought of her mother—she'd had to make a conscious effort to think of her because no one spoke of her and she remembered so little—Ana imagined her as fearless, indefatigable. Free to write her dreams into life. Now, hearing her talk of sleepless nights and the blue hours before dawn, she saw in a flash what Lena must have suffered: the loneliness of being without a family, without a community, without a history.

"You know, when I saw little kids playing at the park in the summer, I'd always see you. The little girls around four, five—because that was how I remembered you. Of course, I'd notice older kids and wonder how you were turning out, what you looked like, what your voice would sound like . . . but it was seeing the little ones that hurt the most. Seeing them with their mothers: eating, crying, having their hair tied back, arguing. The little blond ones especially, but even the ones that didn't look like you. Chinese, Latino, black, whatever. When you've had a child, you start to notice your own child in others . . ."

"A girl called Faith Watson went missing about a year ago," said Ana. "From the neighborhood where we're staying. There are still purple ribbons all up and down the streets."

"My God . . ." Her mother's hand went to her mouth; she shook her head soundlessly. Then, "Her poor parents . . ."

The woman in front of her looked suddenly very small, and Ana bristled with an uncomfortable feeling of pity.

"Why didn't you take me with you?" she asked.

———#———

"I tried to," Lena said. "I got as far as Santa Cruz with you, don't you remember? We waited at the bus stop for hours. Berthold Reimer drove by and saw us and thought we'd been left behind after the market. He offered to bring us back, and there was no way I could say no without causing a scene." She speared a tomato and twisted it in a pool of balsamic vinegar. "On the way home, I thought about what it was going to be like for us. A single mother with no friends, no work, alone in a big foreign city. What would I do with you? It was too dangerous. Better to wait, and send for you when things were more stable."

"But you never did."

"Things never were. Not stable enough, I mean."

"You seem pretty OK now."

"I am, now that you're here. I wish I'd seen that sooner."

———#———

"So why did you leave?"

They were walking back to the station. It was easier to ask questions like this, without needing to look her in the eye. The conversation could stop, and they could just keep walking.

"There are some things . . ." Lena stepped aside to allow a woman pushing a stroller to pass. "Some things that aren't for me to tell you. Things to ask your father."

"That's not fair. You know I can't. And besides, it was you who left."

"I never felt as if I belonged there. I remembered Canada. I hated the heat, the bugs, the crankiness of the grown-ups when Justina and I were little and they were afraid. And I wanted something . . . *more*. I'd always had my doubts, you know. About all those rules, about why we were there. When you were born, that feeling only grew stronger." She shrugged. "Remember, my own father had his falling-out with the ministers over the Penner case—our family didn't exactly have a great history of blending in."

"But you had me. And Papa. And Justina. Something must have happened—" Ana jumped, startled by a car horn. Even after all this time in the city, busy roads still set her on edge. She watched a white car jerk in reverse and speed off down another street, and a second later the stopped traffic began to flow again. She turned back to her mother. "It all happened so suddenly."

"The reasons were complicated. Your father played a part." Lena stopped. "It had nothing to do with you, Ani. It wasn't your fault."

"I know that. You're saying it was his."

"No, I'm not."

"What did he do that was so bad? He hit you?"

"Of course not. Your father would never—"

"Well, then?" Ana forced herself to say it quickly. "You were in love with someone else?"

Lena let out a yelp of laughter. "If only! Look out—" They waited for a bus to turn the corner, its rectangular frame pivoting awkwardly around them.

"There was no one else," she said, as they crossed the street. "Not in that sense."

"How then?"

"Your father's friends . . ."

"Frank Reimer?"

"No, not in the colony." She pulled her hood up as the wind whipped off the water, flinging her hair about her face. "I don't want to get into it, Ani. It's not my story."

"You can't say that." Ana's words were snatched by the wind, lifted high above them, flung out to the lake. "You hurt him too. He didn't ask for this."

"I didn't ask for what he did, either. There's too much to go back to . . ." They had reached the station; she fumbled in her wallet for a token. "One day, we'll talk about it. Not now."

———#———

"Where are you going?"

"To Suvi's." *As usual.* "It's Friday night."

"It's late."

"I'll be back by ten, I promise."

"I'll come and get you."

"Ten thirty, then. *Please.* We have to finish a project for school. It's due on Monday and . . . and Suvi's too busy to work on it this weekend."

"Ten thirty at her front door. I don't want to have to knock."

———#———

"The dance ends at eleven."

"I'll have to leave by ten. You don't have to come."

"Obviously I'll come. You can't just go back to my place and sit on the front step on your own—it's freezing." Suvi leaned closer to the mirror. In the girls' bathroom, cubicle doors slammed open and shut and bodies jostled for space at the counter by the sinks. "You'll still have two hours. That's not bad." She winked at Ana's reflection. "Time for a slow dance, at least."

"With who?"

"Search me. Justin Cook?"

"Don't joke."

Despite the Winter Wonderland theme, few people had bothered with costumes. A few girls turned up with sparkly white tutus and frosted tiaras, but to Ana's eye most people looked dressed for summer: the girls in strapless tops and short skirts, the boys in baggy trousers and T-shirts. Suvi had brought Ana clothes to change into: skinny jeans that kept sliding down her hips and one of Julie's yoga tops, cropped, with a purposely torn neckline and a print of a 1940s bombshell blowing a kiss.

"No one will recognize you," Suvi said. For once, she was wearing a dress—spaghetti straps and a pouffed skirt—but with Converse.

"You look nice."

"You too. Come on—we'll get something to drink first. No way can we be the first ones in."

———#———

Basketball championship pennants flared blue and green and red by a revolving spotlight that roved over the concrete walls, sprung floors and a sea of heads in the sweaty darkness. A hissing dry ice machine spewed clouds at the front of the gym, and on the floor beside the DJ and his decks. The same throbbing beat ran through a succession of songs, wailing electronic voice after voice. Kids skulked along the sidelines, clustered around the drinks table at the back. A troupe of older boys crowded the DJ, bouncing and jostling each other.

"I'm going in," shouted Suvi, and Ana nodded. They found Mischa standing halfway down the gym with another boy, heads bobbing to the music, occasionally shouting in one ear, pointing at someone and grinning.

"Slow dance next," mouthed Mischa to Ana. Then he leaned closer and said, "You want me to hook you up with Sam? You guys have chem together."

Ana shook her head. At least it was dark enough that he wouldn't see the panic burning up her cheeks and throat.

"Come on, Ana!"

"No, I need a drink first. See you outside?"

—⁂—

It was already only a few degrees above freezing, and compared to the heat of the gym the night breeze felt soft and cool. One of the English teachers stood by the coat check inside the front vestibule and waved Ana out. "You can't bring that back in with you," she said, pointing to the plastic cup in Ana's hand.

"OK," said Ana.

"Don't you have a jacket?"

"I'm boiling. I'm just going out for some air."

"Knock yourself out," sniffed the teacher, even as she put out an arm to stop a group of boys from going in with their backpacks. Ana slipped outside past them and made her way to the bench at the foot of the front steps.

Couples came and went. Groups of junior girls swarmed giddily into the building, and the odd lone boy loped up the steps two at a time. As the evening went on, fewer people came out, flooding the quiet stillness with the brief blast of music that followed them from the gym. A group of kids from the year above Ana stood out of the sentry's view by some bushes near the fire exit, the glow of lighters flickering between them. A sweet smell wafted past her, and Ana breathed deeply. She closed her eyes.

"Is it as much fun in there as I'm guessing it's not?" said a voice beside her.

—⁂—

"Those guys over there offer you a puff of their joint?" asked Mr. Peterson.

Ana shook her head.

"Relax. They know that I know that they know. Miss Sykes in

there doesn't. Those kids are just lucky it wasn't Doc Rutter who signed up for this chaperone shift."

He sat down next to her and pulled out a cigarette. "So. What's going on in there?"

"I don't really know. I've been out here mostly."

Mr. Peterson nodded, cigarette tight between pursed lips, frowning as he held up a light. "You don't mind?"

"Go ahead."

He exhaled slowly, extending an arm along the top of the bench. "Not a dancer, then?"

"I'm trying to avoid Karen Spelberg. She thinks I'm after her boyfriend."

Mr. Peterson snorted. "Are you?"

"Of course not. But popular people always assume other people want something they have."

"That's true. Kind of makes you question what it is that makes them popular in the first place."

"It doesn't matter," said Ana. "Suvi says the 'cool girls' will all be fat and divorced with buckets of kids and dead-end jobs by the time they're twenty-five."

"Did she?" Mr. Peterson seemed to weigh this up. "Maybe. Mind you, I knew a few so-called bad girls in high school who ended up at Harvard Law. And some totally forgettable types who are now CEOs. There were also some pretty smug geeks who seemed to assume they'd be the next Bill Gates who are still living in their parents' basements. It works both ways, you know."

"If you say so."

"I do say so." He grinned, took another draw. "Started *Papillon* yet?"

"Yeah. It's good. He's on the ship right now."

"Stuff's about to get worse before it gets better."

"Don't tell me—it will ruin it."

Hands up, smiling surrender.

———#———

"You should get inside," he said at last. "Your lips are turning blue."

"I guess."

"Come on." He dropped the cigarette, squashed it with his heel. Scaled boots, pointed toes. "Or else I'll have to do something, like, totally humiliating and insist on lending you my jacket."

Leather, sheepskin. A musky smell. Cigarettes and something bitter, something sweet.

"OK—I'm going." She stood up. "Does this mean you've finished your shift?"

"I've got to sign off with Syko inside. She'll put the next sap on duty when I've gone. Those kids with the weed had better get moving if they don't want to get caught." He stood up. "After you."

His hand on her back, just above her waist. Julie's top was cropped at an angle; his fingers touched her skin. Warmth against the numbness.

"You have a good night, Ana." He released her to catch the door as it swung open.

Don't go.

"Did you say something?"

She shook her head.

"Maybe give the last dance a try, just for the heck of it," he said. "For me."

---#---

"Why is it always only the gross boys who hit on me?" Suvi pulled a face. She had been late meeting Ana and Mischa to walk home after school and was still flustered. "It's always the ones who smell weird—like, not B.O., but something else. Kind of clammy and vegetable-y."

"Who hit on you?"

"Philip Bird said my hair smelled liked watermelon and did I want to go for burgers at Fran's sometime."

"That's kind of nice."

"Ana, get real."

"Philip Bird's not gross," said Mischa.

"How would you know?" said Suvi.

"Gross is . . . I don't know, like, Sam Greenblatt. That butt-fluff mustache and white stuff in his braces."

"Sam Greenblatt doesn't hit on girls. He's probably gay."

"I don't think so," said Mischa.

They had stopped outside his house. An old man sat on the porch nodding to himself and squinting. Mischa waved to him. "Mr. Shuter," he said to Ana and Suvi, by way of explanation. "He talks to his family in his head a lot. He calls me Bobby."

"That's cool," said Suvi.

"Wanna come in?"

"I've got homework. See you tomorrow?"

"Sure. Bye, Ana."

"Bye."

After they had been walking for another few minutes, Ana said, "Mischa's right. Philip Bird isn't gross."

"*Ana.*" Suvi rolled her eyes. "Of course he said that. Mischa likes Philip. As in, *likes* likes."

"How do you know?"

"I've known him since kindergarten. He knows it. He knows that I know. I don't care if he's gay, but some people do. Why do you think Sean and his gang are always picking on him?"

"I didn't think . . ."

"That's because you're too busy getting picked on by Karen Spelberg."

Suvi stopped and pointed to a stray sock left at the side of the road. She used a stick to pick it up and shove it between the wires on the park fence.

"Mr. Peterson told me kind of the same thing," said Ana. "Well, not really. He said the kids at school will stop picking on each other in a couple of years. I'm not sure, though."

"Of course not. Adults can be totally shitty to one another, right?"

"Yeah."

"Peterson's a dreamboat and all, but he has some wacky ideas," said Suvi. "Sometimes I think he's kind of a drifter. Like, he's still searching for his place in the world. Which is why he's a teacher."

"Teachers can't be drifters," said Ana.

"Sure they can. People become teachers for three reasons." Suvi held up a finger. "One: to feel big. Those are the jerks and the bullies, like Mrs. Hines and Mr. Curtis." She held up a second finger. "Two: because they're genuinely in love with their subject and they want to be, like, missionaries for it. How Miss Sharif is with math." A third finger. "And three: because they don't know what else to do."

She pointed to the pizza place on the corner. "Wanna get a slice?"

"I don't have time. I'm meeting someone in half an hour." Ana saw the question forming in Suvi's face and cut her off before she could ask. "Tutoring."

"Well, have fun."

"Yeah, I won't. See you tomorrow."

—#—

Divide and conquer. Three of the girls staked their place in the line snaking past the sandwich counter—ignoring the older women's sighs and the suited men casting surreptitious glances at the flare of their skater skirts—while the rest commandeered stray chairs to establish a sprawling camp of joined-up tables in the middle of the cafe. A tidal wave of chatter, conditioned hair, glossed lips and chipped nails. Bags in a heap on the floor; jackets piled onto a chair, sliding off, piled up again. The ones who sat shared pictures on their phones, while the ones at the counter ordered milkshakes with grown-up names: ridiculous coffees with whipped cream and chocolate shavings. They flashed shiny debit cards and chewed their lips while punching in newly memorized PIN codes.

Ana watched from a corner, turning her pencil between her fingers so that if anyone caught her eye she could pretend to have been distracted from her work. There was whispering now: hunched shoulders, tense silence, peals of laughter. You'd think they were plotting the greatest comedy coup in the history of time. But no—a representative had been selected to go up to the counter and ask for another cup. The barista was young, muscular, curly-haired. He batted doe-like eyelashes, flashed a Colgate smile. Was he enjoying the attention, or just oblivious to it? These girls probably came in here every day. The girl returned, red-faced, to the table. Slid the cup to her friend, collapsed in a chair while the others squealed their delight.

Is that it? wondered Ana. *She got a cup, not a date.*

Soon after, the subtle social dance of extricating themselves from the group. Having plans, a reason to go and someone to leave with mattered. Ana stared at her notebook and listened.

"OK, I've gotta go meet Alison. Charlie, are you coming?"

"Is anyone going back?"

"My dad's picking me up outside Beck's."

"I'll go back with you, Karen."

"Are you guys staying here?"

"Nah, I'm going with Lindz. Bye, Soph."

Poor Soph, whoever she was. They all got up together, so clearly she must have decided it was safer to depart with the pack and figure out her exit strategy when they got outside. The tables were left scattered with coffee detritus, plastic packaging and crumpled paper napkins. Ana underlined the title at the top of the page. *Athenians and Visigoths.* Surrounded it with stars. Shadowed the letters.

She looked up to see Lena walking toward her. Reaching the table, Lena craned her neck to consider Ana's notebook.

"Hey," she said. "Looks like that essay is coming along great."

———

They got hot chocolates to go, and then they walked to Lena's place. It was smaller than Ana had expected—the ground-floor apartment of a modern three-story building squashed between two bungalows—but pristine. Potted plants on the front steps, shining tiles in the kitchen. Everything—the walls, the counters, the furniture—was white or pale cream. There were no pictures on the walls, but several ferns and a row of squat cacti on the kitchen windowsill. Something about the blankness of it reminded Ana of Mr. Peterson's apartment. As if neither he nor her mother had known how to start over again.

"The bathroom's at the back. There's my room just before it, and the living room here with the kitchen . . . and that's pretty much it."

"Who lives upstairs?"

"Retired couple. Friendly, quiet. And above them, some impossibly hip guy who sits on his balcony playing guitar all summer long. He must be a banker or something the rest of the year."

"It's really nice." Ana thought of Mrs. Fratelli's house with the wire fence and mustard-colored kitchen. "It's smaller than ours, but it's nicer."

"Well, thank you. The tiles reminded me of Bolivia."

"You're right. Speaking of which . . ."

"Here it comes," said Lena.

Ana sat down on the sofa.

"I think you know why we came to Toronto," she said. "I want you to tell me."

"I wish I could, Ani. But I'm not a mind reader. I can only assume your father—"

"No," said Ana. She stood up. "'So long could I stand by, a looker on,'" she said. "You must have known something."

A significant look. "Why don't you tell me what *you* know, instead."

———#———

"I know it had to do with Gerhard," Ana said. "I know he threatened Papa." She took a deep breath. "I know there's a gun at the bottom of the lake."

That got her attention. Lena glanced over her shoulder to check that the door had closed behind them, opened her mouth, glanced down the hallway as if someone might be waiting there, listening. Still she hesitated; Ana could tell she was deciding whether or not to tell her the whole story.

"I know something happened in Moth ten years ago," Ana said. "Just before you left."

Lena paused again. And then opened her mouth to speak.

———— # ————

Once, in a town called Moth, a young man pulled a gun on a police officer and threatened to shoot.

———— # ————

Once, in a town called Moth, a young man pulled a gun on a police officer and fired a warning shot.

———— # ————

Once, in a town called Moth, a young man shot a police officer dead.

———— # ————

"It was a long time ago," Lena said. "I can't be sure that I remember all the details correctly." She waited for Ana to give her permission to stop. Ana said nothing. She sat back down on the sofa.

"It was meant to happen just once," Lena continued. "The first time, I'm not even sure that your father understood what it was he was doing. He was collecting a shipment—produce, we assumed—and taking it to the wholesaler. The colony was halfway between collection points. They would save fuel, I suppose, by paying for him to use a buggy."

"Who were they?"

"Locals. Spanish names I can't remember. Milobo was their nickname for your father, because he drove alone. That was the deal. He told me very little. There was one man with a gold watch—I know, because he gave it to your father. The others were poor."

"So, he took this . . . shipment?"

"Yes. The first time was easy, and he was paid well. Then, a few months later, they asked if he would help again. So he did. The third time they asked, they gave him a gun to keep on him when he went. The road was getting dangerous, they said. Bandits and thieves and gangs. The police were no better; they'd steal and call it bribery, which wasn't even considered a bad word. The most important thing was that he was safe. The next most important thing was that the shipment didn't fall into the wrong hands."

"Only it did?"

"No, it didn't. Your father was as good as his word." Lena breathed deeply. "The handovers happened in Moth. One day, a police car turned up. The officer was alone, totally outnumbered. He pointed his gun at the men who were collecting—the poor ones, the locals—and your father told him to back off. He had the gun ready. The foolish officer didn't retreat, so your father . . . he fired."

"Was Gerhard there? How did he find out?"

"He knew about the extra driving your father had been doing. He's not stupid, Gerhard. The shipments stopped after that, but word spread quickly about the dead officer. He was some important official's son; his murder drew attention. For a while, at least."

"But by then the gun was at the bottom of the lake." Ana swallowed. "The shipments . . . they were coca, weren't they?"

———#———

Ana let the tap run. She'd splashed her face and soaked her arms up to her elbows, and then she dried herself with toilet paper so

Lena wouldn't find a drenched towel on the hanger. She hadn't needed to go to the bathroom; she'd just wanted to be still and quiet and alone.

Her father had blood on his hands. Did Bolivia have a death penalty? That was something they could look up quickly enough on Lena's phone—not that Ana was going to suggest it.

She didn't want to rush to conclusions. She didn't want to think about God or repentance or forgiveness because these were all things that her father must have considered already—and what good had that done, now that they'd fled the country and were living under aliases in a foreign city?

Her mother had known all this time and done nothing. Did this make her a criminal too?

Ana cupped her hands and took two gulps of water before turning off the tap.

Please, please, please, she thought. And then she said it—"Please, please, please . . ."—as the ache in her jaw spread up to her eyes and her temples, and her eyes burned and blurred with tears hotter than those she had shed even as a child in another country, another life.

—#—

Passing by Lena's bedroom on her way from the toilet, Ana hesitated by the open door. The room, like the rest of the apartment, was mostly white—a blank slate. But the bed was covered with a quilt the colors of the lake off Route Four: blue and green with silty grays and a sandy golden border.

The gun been lying in the lake all this time. The same lake into which Lena had dived, fearlessly, after Isaac Buhler. Maybe it was tangled in the same fishing nets that had wound around Isaac's skinny legs. *Isaac Buhler is drowning . . .*

"Who did you make it with?" she asked, when Lena appeared behind her.

"With my sister and my mother when we first arrived in Colony Felicidad," said Lena. "It took us forever to agree on the pattern. It was the first thing we did together to make our house a home."

———#———

It was almost six o'clock.

"Your father will be wondering where you are," said Lena.

"I told him I was going to a prayer group after school." Ana took a sip of camomile tea, placed the mug on the table. "Suvi said I couldn't keep telling him I was at her house because one day he'd come knocking on the door and I wouldn't be there. It was the best thing I could think of."

"What kind of prayer group?"

"He didn't ask. In a way, I don't think he wants to know."

"What does he want, do you think?" Lena leaned forward, studying Ana. "Is he afraid?"

"Maybe. He wants to find you," said Ana. Then, "I don't think he would have come all this way unless it was very serious. He doesn't really want me to be here. Whatever else he could be looking for, I'm not even sure he wants to find it."

———#———

"In that case, why now?" Lena wondered aloud. "Why would Gerhard wait ten years? Something must have happened to make him threaten Miloh now, after all this time."

Ana was quiet for a moment. Then—

"Maria," she said.

Colony Felicidad

It never occurred to me to ask whose it was. It was Maria's baby, obviously: Maria's secret. Then, one afternoon, being careful not to look at me, teasing apart a blade of grass in the shade of the *tipu* tree, Susanna asked if I could guess the father.

There were no young men Maria's age in the colony at that time. Frank Reimer was several years older, and promised to Trude Teichroeb. Everyone knew they were madly in love. There were a few widowers, and Dick Hiebert, who was a bit slow in the head and looked like a boy still, even though he was in his late twenties. I shook my head.

"If I tell you, you must swear not to tell anyone else."

"Of course."

Susanna glanced around to make sure no one was in range to hear. Her little brother, Isaac, had a habit of hiding himself close by to eavesdrop on us—more than once we'd been startled by muffled giggles and had looked up to see him perched at the top of the *tipu* tree, bare feet clenched around the branch like a monkey.

Susanna put her lips almost to my ear.

"*Agustín.*"

I looked at her. "She told you?" Susanna nodded. "Do your parents know?"

"I don't know what she's told Mother. Father may have guessed. He told José that he wanted Ray to help with loading the milk cans from now on, and to hold over Agustín's pay. He daren't say anything, though, or else everybody will know."

"Surely it will be obvious, eventually?"

"Maria has brown hair, and Agustín doesn't have such dark eyes. I think Father is hoping it can be kept a secret."

"Until when?"

"Until he can find the baby another father, I suppose."

Toronto

HIS DOOR WAS CLOSED by the time Ana came in. There was a light on in his room, but no sound.

The next morning, Ana studied her father's hands as he sliced the bread, mixed honey into hot water, turned down the thermostat. They were red and callused, the nails thick and white, clipped so short that the skin puffed around them at the tips. Now, for the first time, she noticed how his right hand trembled when he held anything between forefinger and thumb: a slice of lemon, a switch on the wall. It was almost imperceptible, but it was there.

That was the hand that had held the gun, she thought. *That pulled the trigger, that fired the bullet, that killed the officer.*

She had never seen her father so much as swat a mosquito. He had a temper on him, all right, but he would shout and rage and then retreat into a solitary gloom. He did not break things. He certainly did not strike people.

"Your prayer meeting went on quite late," he said, sitting down to consider a leaflet that had dropped through the letterbox that morning. *Join Your Local Neighborhood Watch*, it said at the top.

"We lost track of time."

"I want you to come home straight after school today," he said. "There's someone I'd like you to meet."

Colony Felicidad

It was not like Gerhard to visit Papa in our house. Perhaps that's why I remember it.

I was sweeping by the back steps when I heard his voice. Papa stepped out to meet Gerhard on the porch, and after exchanging a few words, the two of them went inside. I could hear Papa pour water, the scrape of a chair.

It was wrong to knowingly spy, and so I continued sweeping, following a line down the side of the house past the kitchen window.

Because I had to sweep, I couldn't hear everything. Just scattered words between brush strokes. *Shish-sha, shish-sha.* "Maria . . ." *Shish-sha, shish-sha.* "Delicate . . ." *Shish-sha, shish-sha.* "Time, now . . ." *Shish-sha, shish-sha.* "For you, for Ani . . ."

This went on for a little while before I heard my father stand up and say very clearly that he was not interested. And then, something about Gerhard tidying the mess in his own house rather than spreading it to others.

Gerhard became angry. I could tell by the silence, and then by the scrape of the chair and the sound of a glass hitting the sink. I scuttled back around the side of the house, sweeping furiously.

"You turn this down for your pride," said Gerhard, as he emerged on the porch. "I've never known such foolishness."

"I'm sorry that I can't help."

"The past has a way of finding us out. Maria has learned this. Perhaps you will too."

The night Gerhard fired his rifle into the forest, no one was around to see the wolves scatter. By the time doors and windows clattered open and some of the men rushed outside, Gerhard was standing alone on the driveway. Maria was screaming, leaning from her window with hair loose about her shoulders, and it was some time before her mother was able to draw her indoors and her shouts gave way to sobs.

My father was the first to reach Gerhard, to wrestle the rifle from him. At the time it made no sense: the other men who came out were all carrying guns too, eager to help defend the livestock. Perhaps, also, to defend us.

"Enough!" Papa shouted. "Think about what you are doing."

"Fine words," Gerhard replied, "coming from you."

By then the others had crowded around them, and it was difficult to hear what else was said. And by the time Papa returned to our house, cupping the back of my head in his hand and ushering me inside, several men had headed in to the forest to drive away any wolves that might have lingered on.

In the morning, the boys combed the driveway for wolf tracks, but none were found. Just as they were giving up the search, the first police car arrived.

Toronto

ANA SAW MR. PETERSON standing where he always stood a few minutes before the bell went: leaning against his car at the far end of the parking lot, smoking a cigarette and staring out over the playing fields.

She would tell him. He would understand. He'd read *Papillon*, so he knew about innocent convicts on the run, about the different degrees of sin and redemption. He would know what to do. She could trust him.

She had begun to drift toward him when she heard Mischa call after her. He'd emerged from the gym exit, sketchbook tucked under one arm, apparently unaware of the three boys following him. Before Ana could say anything, Sean had grabbed Mischa in a headlock while Fraser ripped the sketchbook from him and Jack threw his backpack to the ground.

"We're confiscating your porno, freak!" said Sean, pressing Mischa's head closer to the ground.

"Jesus! Look who it is." Fraser had flipped open the sketchbook and brandished a page at Jack.

"Was he drawing me in math again? That's freaking creepy, man—"

"It's not you, butthead. Look . . ."

The three boys paused to consider the drawing more closely, Fraser pinning Mischa to the ground with his knee while Sean clutched the scruff of his neck with both hands. Then Sean ripped the page from the sketchbook and leaped across the parking lot, brandishing it in one hand.

"It's Philip Bird. It's freaking PHIL BIRD!"

By now clusters of students filtering out of the front and side entrances had stopped to watch as Mischa struggled beneath Jack and Fraser, and Sean raced from group to group holding up the picture for all to see.

"He's obsessed. He's been watching this guy, like, forever. Phil! Phil, come over here . . ."

Ana looked around for Suvi, then remembered that she had soccer practice. Across the parking lot, Mr. Peterson was watching the scene intently. Ana saw him register Mischa struggling in the dust and Sean brandishing the drawing at Philip Bird, who had turned bright red at the sight of his portrait. Then he saw Ana. And she could have sworn that he smiled.

Do something, she heard herself say. *You're the grown-up. Do something.*

But Mr. Peterson was too far away to hear, and anyway, he was busy grinding the cigarette into the ground with his heel. Turning his back on the scene, opening the door, climbing into the car, revving the engine.

By the time she'd watched him go, Philip Bird had grabbed the picture from Sean and torn it into pieces.

"Look at me again and die, you pussy," he shouted at Mischa, who was only now brushing himself off, Fraser and Jack having leaped to join the fray at the sight of the picture being shredded. Sean was pulling other pages from the book now, offering them to the crowd like precious signed artifacts.

"Give that back!" Ana heard herself shout, but Mischa's voice cut her off—

"Let them have it."

Seeing him like that, she had found herself stuck for breath.

"Don't say you're sorry," he said to her once everyone had gone. "Don't say anything."

He went home ahead of Ana, having shrugged off her offer of a hand as he got to his feet. They'd silently gathered the pages scattered about the playground, and then Mischa had shoved them all in the garbage can at the corner before tramping off without another word. Ana waited until he had disappeared around the corner before shouldering her bag and slowly making her way toward the street.

She counted the purple ribbons tied along the school fence as she walked. It was now a habit: the more she wished she could shake it, the more impossible it had become. There had been nine before Christmas, but one had disappeared over the holidays.

. . . five . . . six . . . seven.

Ana stopped and turned. She counted them again.

Seven.

Ribbon by ribbon, Faith Watson was fading away.

"Ana," said her father. "This is Sara Toews. She is a friend of your mother's."

The young woman sitting awkwardly on the sofa in the front room smiled warily as she stood to embrace Ana. Her gaze flitted from the girl to her father and back again. "It's so good to meet you at last," she said.

Ana placed her school bag on the floor and looked at her father.

"At last, my work has paid off," he said. "Miss Toews here is going to put us in contact with your mother, and then at last we shall be a family again."

Ana wondered if he realized how ridiculous he sounded. She turned to the young woman.

"Can I get you something to drink?" she said. "Some water?"

Does she know what he did? she wondered. *Is that why she looks so nervous?*

"I can't stay," replied the visitor, who hadn't resumed her seat. She turned to Ana's father. "I can't promise anything. It was several years ago that we shared a room. I'll have to speak to her first, of course . . ."

"Of course, of course! But you know where to find us."

"I do. Good-bye, Ana. It was nice meeting you."

———#———

She flipped her pillow, pressed her cheek onto its cool underbelly. There was nothing to be done about Sara Toews; Lena already knew that Papa was looking for her.

Let them figure it out, she told herself, kicking the sheets down to the edge of the bed only to impatiently pull them back up again. *It's their mess, not mine. I'm just a witness. Collateral.*

And then she remembered what she had seen that afternoon, and heard again those awful words that now sounded less like a defence than a recrimination: "So long could I stand by, a looker on."

When she closed her eyes, there was Mischa's face as Philip Bird tore up his portrait and spat venom at his feet. Despair and humiliation, and something else. Something worse. Recognition? Resignation? As if Mischa wasn't even surprised by his reaction.

She hadn't denied her friend, not obviously—not like Peter denied Jesus—but she hadn't helped him, either.

Ana lay awake until the blue hour, and fell asleep only as the birds began to sing.

———#———

"You were there. You saw what happened. You can give them all detentions—or worse."

"Mischa hasn't come to me, Ana," said Mr Peterson. "If he wanted to register a complaint, that would be another thing."

"Of course he doesn't. He's too embarrassed."

"Perhaps he should have thought of that in advance. Modified his behavior a bit—in the interests of self-preservation."

"His *behavior*?"

"What do you expect? Gay as a garden party in grade nine. Worse things will happen when he's older. I'm not saying it's wrong—"

"Wait." Ana dropped her bag to the floor. "You sound just like one of the ministers at Colony Felicidad. 'It's out of our hands.' 'The Lord's will be done.' Excuses. And meanwhile, people get hurt."

"You're conflating two totally different things, Ana—"

"Just because *you* can't be happy doesn't mean that other people deserve to be unhappy too." She watched him hesitate. "Sometimes I think you *like* that they think I'm a freak, because it means I'll want to hang out with you. And you *like* that they make fun of Mischa because you think it will just prove your theory about how he'll turn into a messed-up adult."

"OK. This conversation is over." Papers shuffled, notebooks slipped into a satchel, keys shaken out of a pocket. "I don't have time to argue with you. I'd suggest you go to the caf and cool down for a bit before your next class."

"You see? That's what's called a double standard. Suvi taught me that. Girls are supposed to be helpless and weak, because in your eyes that makes us attractive; but if a boy is weak, if a boy like Mischa is vulnerable, you shrug and say he's a failure or he has to toughen up, 'modify his behavior.'"

"I'm sorry, Ana." He held the door open. When she didn't budge, he went through it himself. "We're done here."

—#—

"Sara Toews—do you really know her?"

The boardwalk was deserted. The sky over the lake promised a storm.

"We were roommates when I first arrived here." Lena took her hand. "Ani, it's OK. She called me this morning and told me what your father had to say."

"She was in our living room. You're going to have to decide pretty fast what you're going to tell Papa."

"I know that. Sara's discreet, though. Let me worry about it, OK?" The first droplets of rain flicked against their cheeks. "Come on—there's a bandstand in the park. Let's not get struck by lightning like complete idiots in the meantime."

They took cover as branches rustled darkly, rain spitting against the leaves like bullets. Ana dropped onto the bench in the bandstand, digging her fingernail into the grooves where someone had carved JA + MD 4 EVA.

"What did Sara tell you? About Papa, I mean. What does he want?"

— # —

"She says he needs to be sure I won't come back."

"To Colony Felicidad? Why?"

"Gerhard reacted badly to the news about Maria. According to your father, it drove him to a breaking point. He developed some crazy scheme to blame the pregnancy on your father and get him to accept responsibility for her and the baby. Papa had no wife and a secret that Gerhard was willing to exploit. Gerhard threatened him." Lena breathed slowly. "He threatened both of us. You too. That's why your father left in such a hurry. He didn't want any of us to be hurt."

"But . . ." It made sense—awful, cruel, cold-headed sense. A tumult of thoughts poured through Ana's mind, but only one of them rang clear and true.

"Maria's baby would have been born by now."

— # —

Two days later: the first golden, barefoot-on-the-front-porch afternoon of the year. Little kids rode their scooters in circles around the cul-de-sac in front of Lena's building. Dogs pranced, tongues lolling out of the sides of their mouths. For the rest of the city, today was a beginning.

"What are you thinking about all of this?"

Lena shook her head. "I don't know."

Ana dug her toes into the gravel path.

"What will happen next?" she asked. "With you and me and Papa."

"How am I supposed to even begin to process that question?"

"You left him once before."

"That was survival. That was escaping a community that I didn't belong to anymore. A place that wasn't just restricting me, but was becoming dangerous too—for both of us. Escaping what could have been the disgrace of a murder trial, exclusion . . ."

"If you'd really loved him, you would have stayed."

"It wasn't that simple. If he'd gone to prison we'd have been on our own and things would have been hard for you. I'd already decided that I didn't belong there—but you were just a child, and I knew Justina would look after you."

"Papa loved *you* enough to come all the way out here to make sure you were safe."

"He loved *you* enough to leave Bolivia. He was worried about you because of what Gerhard threatened."

"You could move in with us now."

"Have you lost your mind?"

They watched an elderly couple make way for a mother with a stroller. Greetings were exchanged; the old man fluttered his fingers at the baby.

"Obviously, you're not going back there."

"Obviously?" Ana rankled. "How do you know?"

"What a silly question. *I'm your mother,* Ani."

———#———

"You don't even *know* me."

"Oh, don't give me that teenage baloney." Lena blew air between pursed lips and batted her hand. "I know stuff about you that even you don't know. I know that you spent the first night of your life throwing up black bile that made me wonder if I'd given birth to a demon. I know that you were born with a head of dark hair that fell out within a month and grew back blonde and fuzzy at the back where your head rubbed against your mattress. I know that when you were a toddler, in the summertime you liked nothing better than pulling off your clothes and running naked through Gerhard Buhler's garden. Your father would go bright red, but secretly I'm pretty sure he enjoyed it—"

"Those are all things from long ago. You don't know who I am *now*."

"Is that so? Well, then." She folded her arms. "Please. Enlighten me."

"This is stupid."

"I'm waiting, Ani." A pause. "Or are you pushing back like this because really, if you're honest, you don't have the slightest idea, either?"

———

"Tell me this," said Lena. "Which do you prefer? Ani in Colony Felicidad, or Ana in Toronto?"

"I'm the same person, though."

"Are you?" Lena shrugged and pulled her lip. "I'm not."

"You can't change who you are inside."

"Maybe not. But that's not to say that you *don't* change."

Ana picked up a piece of gravel and tossed it at an empty flowerpot. It bounced off the rim and fell to the ground with a clatter. "Well, then—which you do *you* prefer?"

"If it weren't for missing you, I would say this Lena. Lena here. But it wasn't always that simple. It took me a few years to be sure."

"So how am I supposed to be able to answer that question now?"

"What does your gut tell you?"

Ana picked up another piece of gravel, pressed its uneven points with her thumb. "I don't know. I feel free here, but that's not always a good thing. Sometimes . . . it's weird."

Lena nodded. "Uh-huh . . ."

"I like school sometimes. The idea that I can do anything when I graduate. I would never have that freedom at home. I like the library and the stores and being able to go places by myself." Ana tossed the piece of gravel at the flowerpot. This time it landed soundlessly on the barren soil inside. "I feel like my life is moving forward here."

More nodding.

"But then in other ways it feels less free. I miss the fields and being alone—I mean, properly alone, not just on my own but surrounded by strangers. Sometimes I think the things we learn here are really . . . artificial. Kids don't learn to make as many decisions on their own. Their parents do so much for them . . ."

"You think so?"

"They grow up differently. In some ways, Suvi knows so much more than I do about . . . everything. But in other ways, she's really young still."

"So, are the old ways better?"

"Not better, just different."

"For you, I mean."

Ana picked up another piece of gravel.

"I'm not sure," she said. She let the gravel drop from her hand. "Maybe the things that are better are things you can take with you anywhere, though."

Lena bumped Ana's knee with hers. "You might be on to something there."

"I should go. Suvi's expecting me to stop by on my way home."

———✦———

She told Suvi about the fight, about Mr. Peterson and how Mischa didn't want to talk about it.

"Leave him alone for a few days, and he'll be fine. He doesn't want anyone feeling sorry for him," said Suvi. "It's always like this."

"It isn't fair."

"Tell me about it."

They'd walked across the bridge and through the ravine, not minding the time or where they were going. Before they knew it, they were on his street.

"We can just walk by," said Suvi. "He's probably having dinner now, anyway. His parents are strict about that."

It was the hour when the insides of houses became visible: lighter inside than out. The huge sash curtains were still open in the bay window, and a lamp was lit on the piano in the parlor. An old man sat on the porch, the front door open beside him. Upstairs, a hand drew blinds on a bedroom window. There was a smell of soup, and a clatter of dishes, and above this the sound of music. An orchestra, a crooning voice.

"Look," said Suvi, stopping by a tree and pulling Ana close.

Two figures were moving in the parlor: one tall and stooped, with cloud-shaped hair, the other small-boned and upright. A woman and a boy. They danced slowly, and as they turned, Ana could see the smile on the old lady's face as Mischa said something to her. They covered the length of the room, skirting the piano, and as the music ended the old lady dropped a creaking curtsy.

A voice interrupted the dancers; both figures turned and disappeared into the dining room at the back of the house.

"It'll be dark soon," said Suvi. "We'd better go."

⸺⸺

"It's too late for you to still be out. You have school in the morning."

"I'm not still out. I'm home now."

"Don't try to be clever."

"Perhaps I don't want to risk coming home to some strange

woman sitting on our sofa, just for you to say we're going to be a family again. Perhaps I'd rather just skip all of that, you know?"

—#—

"Enough," said Papa. "That is enough, Ani."

"Stop telling me what to do."

"I will tell you, and you will listen!"

"Why?"

"Because I am your father!"

"You were a *drug runner*. What's a couple of shots at a party and a walk through the ravine compared to selling cocaine?" Ana watched his expression fall, couldn't stop herself from turning the knife. "Or killing a police officer?"

Her father's face turned gray. For a moment she thought perhaps he might lunge at her, or have a heart attack and keel over onto the floor. Then he just said, "Go to your room. Now. Before I do something I might regret."

Ana was happy to get out of there, but she didn't go to her room. She ran out the front door and went straight to Suvi's house.

—#—

"Jesus," said Suvi. "*Crack*?"

Ana hadn't planned to tell her—but as soon as she opened the door she'd started to cry, and once they were up in Suvi's room everything came flooding out.

"This is crazy," Suvi said. "Like, holy shit. He killed someone? He was running drugs?"

"I don't think he knew that's what it was. And he hadn't meant to shoot. It was practically self-defence."

"OK. OK. We can work this out . . ." Suvi slid off her bed and began pacing up and down. "You could come and live here. Julie and Steve could, like, adopt you . . ."

"But I've got parents. They're just . . ."

"Seriously messed up."

Ana fiddled with one of the tassels on Suvi's bedspread. "Maybe I could move in with her."

"Lena? I thought things were weird between you."

"Suvi, there's weird and there's drug-running and murder weird."

"OK." Suvi sat on the chair by her dressing table, backward, and leaned her chin on her elbows. "What will happen to him, do you think?"

"I don't know. If he goes back there, he could be arrested. But he doesn't want to stay here. He's kind of stuck." Ana pulled a cushion onto her lap and doubled herself over it. "I can't believe he lied for so long."

"He didn't lie, though. He just didn't tell you." Suvi waited. "Like you didn't tell me about Peterson."

"That's completely different!"

"OK, fine. But your dad's not the only one. You haven't told him that you found your mother, have you? You've kept that from him." Suvi ignored the noise of exasperation that Ana made into the cushion. "Don't kill me for saying this, but . . . I kind of feel sorry for him. You know?"

—*—

She returned to the house the following morning, on the way to school, to collect her bag. Suvi waited on the curb.

"Ani." A voice from the kitchen. "Ani, please."

Her father's eyes were ringed; his shoulders slumped. He wore the same clothes he'd had on the night before.

"I'm going to be late for school. Isn't that what you were worried about?"

"This cannot go on. We have lost too much already."

Ana folded her arms.

"I know what this is about," he continued. "You're unhappy. We should go back. I should never have brought you here—"

"Wait a minute." Ana uncrossed her arms. "You mean to say that after coming all this way, dragging me along with you, you want to take me back there?"

"This is not our home."

"Neither is Colony Felicidad—not now, not after everything that happened with Gerhard Buhler. Even if the colony doesn't give you up, the Bolivian police will throw you in jail for the rest of your life. And Suvi says Mama and I could go to jail too, as accessories to the crime—whatever that means. Because we know about *it* . . . about what you did." Ana watched him dig a groove into the table with the sharp edge of a broken plastic pen, thought of him hunched there late at night with his paint tray and fine brushes. Diamonds and helixes and staircases leading nowhere. "We can't live there, and now you don't want to stay here. It's almost like you're *trying* to make our life impossible."

"I brought you here for your own safety."

"And now I want to stay."

He put his head in his hands, took a deep breath, and then looked up.

"Who told you all of this? About Gerhard. About . . ." He swallowed. Ana bit her lip. *He's afraid of finding her too.*

"She did," she said.

————————#————————

"He wants us to go back." Ana didn't look at Lena. "Me and him."

"That's insane. Go back to what, exactly?"

"That's what I said."

"No way. He can't just parachute you into my life like this and then take off!"

Ana pushed past her down the hallway, helped herself to a lemonade from the fridge.

"Take off like you did, you mean?" she said.

Lena followed her into the kitchen.

"You know that's not fair," she said. She watched Ana sit down at the table. "There are ginger snaps in the cupboard," she said.

"No, thanks. I can't stay for long, anyway."

Lena pulled out another chair.

"You don't seem particularly fazed by this idea," she said. "This Bolivia thing."

"He doesn't mean it. He can't. There's nothing for us to go back to. It would be suicide for him, and that would mean all sorts of trouble for me. We don't have any money, anyway . . ."

"So you don't want to leave?" Lena stretched her arms across the table, taking Ana's wrists in her hands. Ana recoiled. There was fear in her mother's eyes.

"I like my friends. I've only just begun to figure things out here . . ."

"And what about me?"

Suddenly her mother was transformed: a shell built of a thousand broken pieces. The slightest tap would set her crumbling. Ana set her glass on the table.

"What do you mean? No, hold on." She pushed the glass away. "Look, nothing has changed. We survived without you for ten years. You don't need to worry about us."

"That's not what I meant. I meant . . . oh God, this is going to sound so selfish . . ."

Ana waited.

"Just one thing," said Lena. "One question. I need to know."

————

"You know what I realized?" Suvi collapsed backward into the mildewed beanbag chair, aiming a rubber band out the tree house window. It was the first time since the fall that it was warm enough for them to be up here again, and everything smelled a bit damp and neglected.

"That there are ants coming out of that beanbag?" said Ana. Suvi glanced down to where she'd pointed at the split in the seam and flicked at one of the scurrying black dots before returning to fiddling with the elastic.

"I realized that my attachment to my parents is based entirely on material stuff and advertising," she said.

"What does that mean?" said Mischa.

"It means my mother and I have our best times when we're out shopping together or going to movies or going out for sushi—basically, *consuming* stuff—and Steve and I have our best times together watching sports. As in, watching guys who get paid millions of dollars to hit a ball with a stick, and then stuffing our faces with overpriced processed meat in buns as long as your arm, which is why most North Americans are overweight, and staring at loads of ads for stuff we don't need and making jokes about the guy who voices the razor commercials."

"What's wrong with that?"

"What's wrong is that I wouldn't know how to talk to them otherwise. Like, if you sat me in an empty room with Julie, and there was no food and no TV and no shopping—what would we talk about? And Steve would be even worse. He'd, like, try to tell me about his childhood and impart some deep life lesson."

"That doesn't sound so bad," said Ana.

"But it never happens, right? We never talk about real stuff. I mean, we talk about kids starving in Africa and why politicians are sleazebags and the craziness that stores can't just add taxes straight onto price tags . . . but we don't talk about *us*."

"Why would you even want to?" said Mischa.

Suvi shrugged. "I don't know. I feel like I should."

Ana flicked open her Coke and teased the metal tab back and forth. When it had broken off she handed it to Suvi, who was collecting them to make a bracelet like one she'd seen a girl at school wearing.

"Lena wanted to talk about *us* last night," said Ana. "It was weird. In the end, she came right out and asked if I loved her."

"Oh my God. What did you say?"

"I said I didn't know."

"Ouch," said Mischa.

"How can you love someone you've only just met?" Ana protested.

"Jessica Alvarez says she's been in love with Mike Gibson since the first time she saw him at the book sale," said Suvi. "They've been dating for five months now."

"That's IN love," said Ana. "That's different."

"Your mother left you," said Mischa. "She can't expect you to love her. You earn it, right? By looking after your kids. And if you let them down, you have to earn it back."

"That's kind of harsh," said Suvi.

"What's harsh is the old people who live in my parents' house and call me little Billy or little Joey or little Frank or whatever because their own kids never bring their grandchildren to visit."

"But some of them have dementia," said Suvi. "That's different."

"Yeah, but not all of them. Some of them are just fine, and they know that their kids never visit them."

"What would you do, Ana?" said Suvi. "If your mother was really old and dependent and stuff—would you visit her?"

Ana rested the Coke can against her knee, enjoying the sensation of cool metal pressed against her first mosquito bite of the summer. "I don't know," she said. "She survived without me for long enough, so why not?"

"But you like her."

"Yeah."

"Well, that's a start."

———※———

At last, an agreement to meet. In the conference room at First Light: a tiny, carpeted seminar space in the basement that wasn't booked for use for another two days.

"So we'll have all the time in the world," Lena joked to Ana before they parted.

"How was it?" Ana asked her father that evening. She waited until after he'd come in, gone upstairs, returned with hair freshly rinsed and combed. Bright-eyed, but silent.

"Your mother has not changed," he said.

—#—

The next time, a week later, Lena came to their house. Ana observed her taking in the scuffed carpet, the mold patch on the bathroom ceiling, the cabinet door hanging off its hinge in the kitchen, with the same blandly interested smile that betrayed neither disgust nor pity.

"May I see your room?" she asked Ana.

"Of course—it's right up this way."

Over nine months, the detritus of teenage life had cloaked her room in a veil of normality: clothes, books, upended book bag. No computer, no music, no posters—but the Polaroid of her with Lena was stuck to the window, next to some photo-booth snaps with Suvi and Mischa.

"It's nice."

"Does it smell to you? When we first moved here, I thought it smelled really weird."

"I don't smell anything. Nothing bad, anyway. Deodorant, maybe?"

"That's OK, then."

"I guess we should go back down. Your father's waiting."

—#—

"So those are the ribbons you mentioned," Lena said, as Ana walked her to the front gate.

Ana nodded. "There used to be a lot in front of school. Yesterday I counted three."

Her mother hesitated, and then she took Ana in her arms and squeezed her so tightly Ana thought she might snap in two.

"I'm sorry," said Lena into her hair. "I'm so, so sorry."

—⁂—

Lena invited them to dinner at her house the following night. After she had left, Ana realized that she must have registered the bare cupboards and scaled kettle in the kitchen, the cut-price chicken in the fridge and the bowl of Weetabix that her father had been snacking on when she'd arrived.

"We have so much more to talk about," her mother said on the doorstep as Ana handed over her jacket. *So much more?* Ana found herself thinking. *More* implied that they'd talked already, but her father had hardly said a thing, and all the conversation the night before had mainly been to do with Mrs. Fratelli and the saga of the broken furnace.

A spicy-sweet smell welcomed them in Lena's hallway: a primary layer of something smoky or barbecued, and over it the sizzle of chili, the frying of onion and garlic, the sweetness of fruit. The kitchen windows were completely steamed up and Lena glided from counter to counter gathering fistfuls of chopped parsley, half a lemon squeezed through her fingers, a bowl of diced almonds.

"Help yourselves to drinks," she said over her shoulder. "There's juice and tea and water. The milk's probably past its best."

Ana poured water for her father and herself. "Can I help?" she asked.

"It's all done. That's the beauty of curry."

"Indian curry?"

"I hope that's OK?"

Ana looked to her father. "We've never tried it before."

"I'm sure it will be delicious," he said quickly.

"I didn't make it hot," said Lena hurriedly. "The first one I ever tasted almost blew my head off, and it would have been the last if

Sara hadn't dragged me to this great little place on Gerrard Street and made me try some other dishes. Vegetable *biryanis* and *saag paneer*—that's spinach with cheese—and *popadoms*. Oh, and the chutneys! Not so different from the pickles I used to make with Justina . . ." She trailed off, wiped her cheek with her arms. "You know, it's crazy, but I spent most of today trying to talk myself out of it. 'They'll hate it; it's totally unlike what we'd usually eat. Why make things harder when everything's already complicated enough?'" Her voice was jokey, but she was watching Ana's father with a worried intensity. "And then I thought, 'Hang on, how long have they been here? And this food is amazing. It's my favorite, actually. They're brave; they're adults'"—a look thrown at Ana—"'they'll cope.' Better than that, I hope. It's just a *korma*, the mildest kind. Like a lovely creamy stew. It's the first thing I tried when I went back to that restaurant, and the first thing I made when I decided to try cooking something new."

Ana looked at her father. He was listening intently, watching her mother with a mixture of curiosity and awe.

"We aren't afraid of a little challenge," he said. "Are we, Ani?"

"No. It smells great."

"Well, if all else fails there's cheese and toast." Lena pulled the dishcloth from her belt and tossed it onto the counter. "Come on, let's sit in the living room while this finishes."

—#—

"School will be winding down soon."

"In a few weeks."

"Will you miss it?"

Lena's question hung in the air as Ana piled the plates.

"It will be nice to have a break over the summer," Ana said. Then, avoiding her father's eye, "And to be in grade ten next year. You know, not at the bottom of the heap anymore."

Silence. Lena emptied her glass and reached for the stack of plates.

"Well," she said. "I can understand that."

"It's been good for her," said Ana's father. Mother and daughter looked at him in surprise. "Listen to her English," he said. "And the sums she can do are impressive. Some of it makes me nervous. I find myself wondering what the application will be, how far it will take her away from the important things—but it hasn't changed her. It only shows how smart she is. That's God's gift, isn't it?"

This was more than Ana had heard her father speak in many months.

"So . . ." she began. "Does that mean we're staying?"

"I didn't say that."

Her heart sank. Of course the evening could never have gone that well; of course it would all come tumbling down now . . .

"But what a shame to leave now," said Lena in a small voice. "When it's going so well."

"There have been problems too. Insolence, disobedience." He shook his head. "You haven't been there. You haven't seen it."

Ana took the plates into the kitchen and rinsed them in the sink. Her father had asked for a second helping of Lena's curry, which, although like nothing Ana had ever tasted, made her feel strangely warm and full and contented.

The neighbor's cat was sitting outside the kitchen window, sniffing the air, its tail flicking impatiently. Ana picked up a leftover piece of chicken from the pot, wound open the window and nudged it onto the ledge.

She returned to find her father with his hands on his knees, nodding at the floor.

"Your mother says you need stability," he said. Ana waited. "And she may be right."

Ana and Lena exchanged glances. Registering them, her father stood up.

"We have stayed long enough," he said. "It's late."

"Papa," said Ana. "Don't forget."

He paused, then disappeared into the hallway where he'd left a plastic bag. Inside was a cereal box. He returned with the box and handed it to Lena.

"It's nothing," he said. "A silly thing. But Ana insisted."

They watched in silence as Lena carefully tipped the wooden blocks onto the table.

"They're beautiful," she said. Then, studying them more closely, "Six sides. Six puzzles?" He nodded. "My goodness. I'll be up all night trying to put it together."

Ana could have been mistaken, but she was sure her father smiled then.

"We can always help you with it," she said.

---#---

Closing the kitchen cupboard, Ana noticed it. A glancing movement, a skein of substance, vanishing soundlessly behind the sugar bowl.

She waited, heart thudding. She knew that it wasn't a mouse. A mouse wouldn't have frightened her. It wasn't a ghost, either.

Gingerly, she picked her way across the floor and reached for the dustpan in the corner. She extended it toward the counter, using the edge to make contact with the sugar bowl. No sooner had she nudged it to one side, out the creature flashed—eight legs scrambling hairily over the laminate surface, slipping, skidding, intent on escape—and Ana let out a yelp.

The noise seemed to stun it. It froze, crouched, by the edge of the sink, legs drawn up high against its long, brown body.

It waited. Ana waited.

"Is that you, amigo?" she whispered at last.

The spider didn't move. Ana retreated toward the fridge and opened it. Pulled out a few lettuce leaves and a broccoli floret. Placed them on a paper towel at the other end of the sink, by the open window.

"Your favorite," she said. "Just remember our deal. Stay out of my room."

---#---

"The Lennon sisters," said Ana. She pointed at Lena's phone. "Can you show me?"

It took a few seconds for Lena to get to YouTube.

"'Mister Clarinet Man' . . . 'Que Sera, Sera' . . . hang on, let me find the one . . .'"

Four sisters in grainy black and white on a variety show stage. Peter Pan collars, high-waisted skirts, crimped hair in ponytails; the youngest, still a child, in a boxy tunic with short bangs. Sweet smiles, clear voices, perfect harmonies. Ana cut a glance at her mother, who was mouthing the words along with them as she watched.

Although we're apart
You're part of my heart
And tonight you belong to me.

The song swung into a free-wheeling third verse, and Lena smiled at Ana.

"I know, it's old-fashioned," she said. "But you've got to admit, they're pretty good."

———#———

"Bedtime for me," said Lena at ten. "I know it's early for a sleepover, but I'm bushed."

"That's OK. I'm going to read for a bit."

"You can leave the bathroom light on if you want." She blew a kiss from the doorway. "Night, night."

She must have been more tired than she'd realized. When next Ana opened her eyes, the book lay on the floor by the sofa and the room was in darkness. She moved her head a quarter turn and registered a light on in the kitchen.

Footsteps. The sound of the fridge opening, closing. Running water. A light switched off. A pause in the hallway, steps retraced.

Ana closed her eyes and turned her face back into the pillow.

She heard her mother take a breath in the doorway, hold it. How long was she going to stand there? The floor creaked as she stepped closer to the sofa. Set her glass gently on the floor. Pulled something off the armchair. The blue quilt. It smelled musty and sweet: laundry detergent mixed with something lingering. The floor creaked again as Ana felt a blanket gently lowered onto her shoulders, straightened so that it covered the length of her.

Lena stood there a moment longer, then carefully picked up the glass and tiptoed back to the hallway. After a second her door closed, and Ana opened her eyes once more in the dark.

—*//*—

The school fair officially opened with the Dance Crew delivering a thumping routine on a temporary stage. Or rather, the Dance Crew miming backup to Karen, who, in Ana's mind, would be turning cartwheels in perpetuity in that measly leotard.

Mr. Peterson was watching from the sponge-throw on the other side of the pitch, a smile teasing his lips. All of the teachers were wearing normal summer clothes, and he'd turned up in long shorts that showed his legs, tanned and covered in a thicket of hair, and a barbed wire tattoo around one ankle.

"Save me a popsicle," Ana told Suvi. "I'll see you at the lunch tree in a minute."

Mr. Peterson smiled as she approached, and he held out a wet sponge. "Take your pick. Miss Hines or Mr. Hamza."

"I don't have a ticket."

He winked at her. "This one's on the house."

"It's OK." Ana rooted in her backpack and then returned the dog-eared paperback and yellowing comic to him in a plastic bag.

"Oh . . ." The other teachers were a good distance away, bored behind the wooden cutout. There were no other kids in line. Mr. Peterson considered the bag. "I hope you enjoyed them."

"Thanks."

Nearby, a little girl was having her face painted by one of the student volunteers. Orange and black and white stripes, a pink nose. The child held very still, staring into the eyes of the older girl who would turn her into a tiger, concentrating hard on becoming what she couldn't yet see.

"You'll be in Miss Simon's class next year," said Mr. Peterson. "I've recommended you."

Ana nodded.

"I'm sorry things have ended like this," he continued. "I feel . . . let down . . ."

"I didn't let you down," she said. "I grew up."

He blinked, and then he smiled, and opened his mouth to reply.

"I've got to go," she said. "My friends are waiting for me."

Colony Felicidad

Poor old Tomas de Molli. You'd think it would be pretty thrilling having a town named after you, but not if they got your name wrong. That would be worse than nothing, like being given a present only to have it snatched away a minute later.

I used to wonder what happened to Tomas. Then I'd get to thinking about what might have happened to Popi. (Sue, I suppose, being a dog, would have met a typically doggy end long before the others.)

The porcelain works obviously never came to much, but I like to think that Tomas stayed in his village in the saltpeter field until the very end. Moth was where his dream had been born and flickered and foundered and faded. Long after the last families trundled off to try new lives in Potosí or Oruro or maybe even La Paz, old Tomas would stay in his little white house with his adopted Guaraní son.

By the time Tomas died, Popi would have been a young man dressed in European clothing. Too big to swing on the bell-pull in the church or throw marbles up against the well in the town square. It would have been the end of one century and the beginning of a new one by the time he had to decide whether to stay in Moth like Tomas—journeying for days to the nearest town for butchered meat and cheese and anything that he couldn't grow in his vegetable patch, which was most things—or start all over somewhere else.

Maybe he was even tempted to go back to his village in the hills, assuming it was still there. At some point he might have learned to chew coca and speak the old language. I thought it was doubtful, though. It's hard to go back when so much has changed around you, and even more so when you yourself have changed so much.

Toronto

"YOU'RE STAYING?"

"For now, at least. There's still a lot they have to work out . . . but, yeah. I think so."

"This calls for a celebration," said Suvi, leaping from the front step. "Pancakes at Chewey's? I've got fifteen bucks. Meesh?"

"Ten. We can do two plates between us, and shakes."

"Woot!" Suvi flung an arm around each of her friend's shoulders and swung off of them like a monkey. *We'll AL-ways be to-GETH-er . . . shoo-bop-a-shooby-doo . . ."*

"You're crazy," said Ana.

"There are drugs that can take care of that." Suvi jabbed her in the ribs. "On the other hand, you'll always be Menno."

───────

"This summer is going to be epic."

"Just normal would be fine."

"Yeah, but we should aim for better than fine." Suvi slurped her milkshake and mopped up the last drops of maple syrup with a giant pancake slice. "These are the important years, right? The years that determine if you're going to be this faded star for the rest of your life, or if you're always going to have a chip on your shoulder about never making the basketball team, or if you'll hold on to your insecurity about how you look because some bitch called you Big Nose in the changing room."

"Great," said Mischa.

"It *is* great! Because there's still time for us to decide not to be freaks, and not to be jerks, and not to be total recluses, so that we have some cool stories to tell our grandkids . . . but mainly so that we can just live with ourselves when we're older, you know?"

"If you say so."

"She's right," said Ana. "It's kind of cool, if you think about it."

"Anything's possible," said Suvi. "Anything."

—#—

Walking home past the school that afternoon, Ana sensed that something was wrong. The school building stood dark and still, the windows stripped of displays and notices and wall charts, the parking lot eerily empty. But that wasn't it.

Then, running a hand along the iron railing, she realized that the last of the purple ribbons had gone. Untied in the end-of-year cleanup, perhaps, or simply weathered away by months of wind and snow and rain.

Ana stood there for several moments, unable to move. Then she remembered the scarf that Lena had bought her all those months ago in Kensington Market. Ana hadn't worn it once; she kept it tied to her bag instead.

She went home and told her father that she would be back again in ten minutes. She ran upstairs, pulled her bag from the bed. Untied the scarf. Back downstairs, down the street, running now, running . . .

Ana looped the scarf around the center railing: once, twice, three times. Knotted it. Wrapped it one more time and double-knotted it again.

"For Faith," she said. "Wherever you are."

—#—

They had dinner again the following week at Lena's. This time, she and Ana cooked one of Justina's recipes: lamb chops, yellow rice, corn and peas. It tasted, they all agreed, exactly as it always had at Justina's table. Perhaps even better.

Papa told a story about one of Mrs. Fratelli's grown sons locking himself in the garage by accident and having to call the fire department to cut the door out. They had laughed and shaken their heads at his idiocy. Lena said that her work was moving into a new office and everyone was on edge because most of the files had been packed up and some of the important ones weren't accounted for. Ana told her parents about Suvi's plans to take her to the CNE, which was all about rides and music and cotton candy. Ana still had no idea what cotton candy tasted like.

"Pink and fluff," said Lena. "Unless it's blue. Then it's blue and fluff."

Ana smirked. "So, it tastes of fluff?"

"Sweet fluff. It turns to air in your mouth."

When the dishes were done, her father said, "Ana, your mother and I need to talk."

So Ana took her backpack to her mother's bedroom at the far end of the apartment, closed the door and, with a sigh of contentment, lay down on the bed.

When she woke, the room was dark. Voices elsewhere in the apartment rose and fell, separated by silences and footsteps.

Ana opened the bedroom door to find the hallway in darkness. Her parents were in the living room. The door was closed.

"Too much . . . let's just . . . time . . ." Lena's voice was low, tired.

"There's been enough time."

Ana crept farther down the hallway.

"Do you realize what you did to us?" her father was saying. Ana couldn't hear Lena's reply. "She was never the same child. This is all new. This is all down to you."

At first Ana thought there was accusation in his voice—it was urgent, energized—but then she realized it was something else.

"You underestimate yourself," said Lena.

"You know it as well as I do. I was never enough for her. How could I be?"

"What more could you be?"

A long silence. Ana crept closer to the door.

Her father did not reply.

Ana returned to the kitchen, switched on the light. One by one, she took the dishes that had dried on the rack and returned them to the cupboards. Eventually, the noise would bring them back to her.

———✦———

"Papa?"

Two packed bags sat at the bottom of the stairs.

"Papa? I'm back."

She'd said good-bye to Suvi for the week—she and her parents were going to New York to see relatives. Suvi had asked Ana to come, but Ana told her they still had catching up to do, time to spend together as a family.

"What's with the bags?" Ana fumbled with one of the zips, caught a peek of her father's blue shirt. She checked the other bag. Her toothbrush, the Camp Kawinpasset sweatshirt. "What's happening?"

"It's time, Ana. We have to go." Her father appeared in the kitchen doorway, wiping his hands on a towel. He didn't look at her.

"Go where? What are you talking about?" Ana frowned. "Are we moving in with Mama?"

Her father glanced up. Two smears of red colored his cheeks. "I can't, Ana. It's too much. Everything has happened so quickly. It's not for her to decide what we do—"

"But everything is going so well . . ."

"For you, perhaps, it might seem that way. I even found myself thinking that she is what you need right now. But she lives here; she wants a different life. You are too young to make that decision." He raised his hand, stopping her. "I am too old for this. Things falling through my fingers, others telling me what to do. We made a mistake coming here . . ."

"Where then? Where are you going?"

"Perhaps to Johan's. Would you like that?"

"To visit, maybe. But why are we taking everything?" She went into the kitchen. The cupboards had been stripped. "What's going on?"

"New tenants are moving in. I think it's a sign. If God had wanted us to stay, he would have made it easier."

Ana shook her head.

"Oh, no," she said. "I'm not leaving. Have you spoken to Mama about it?"

"It's not easy for us to speak at the moment. There's been too much speaking, perhaps."

"What is that supposed to mean?" She felt her eyes prickle, grow hot with tears. "What are you trying to do to us?"

"I only want what's best for you—"

"And running away again is best?" Ana coughed a laugh. "That's what she did, and so you think that's what you can do? Twice?" She picked up the bag packed with her things. "Well, look, there's another person in this family who can do it too. I'm finished with chasing after her and being pushed around by you!"

"Ana, wait—listen to me . . ."

"I've listened. Go and sit in church and tell it to God if it makes you feel better. You've always preferred Him to us, anyway."

She hauled the bag across the threshold and slammed the front door behind her. As she hurried down the flagstone path, bag banging against her hip, she waited for the sound of the opening door, his voice calling after her.

She waited until she reached the street, and when still it didn't come she continued on into the gathering dusk.

Colony Felicidad

When my mother left, I pretended not to hear the whispers. Not allowing myself to hear anything bad was all part of being good—and I had to be good, or else whatever was out there, beyond the forest, would come for me too.

When I was little, I couldn't understand why someone would choose to leave Colony Felicidad. We had everything we could want, and we lived according to God's will. That only meant one thing: if my mother hadn't left willingly, she must have been spirited away by the Devil.

It had happened before, and it could well happen again—people left colonies from time to time, and there was no stopping them—but when it did, it made those of us who'd been left behind cling even closer together, like survivors on a storm-tossed ship.

Toronto

THERE WERE DIFFERENT SPIRITS living in the ravine, not like the *pombéro*. The First Nations people here had worshipped different gods, had different devils. In history, Ana's class had been shown an early map of the city charting suspected tribal burial sites. There was one under the tennis courts near Thandi Rosen's house, and several dotted at various points along the river.

Ghosts can't cross running water, Ana told herself. Then she hesitated, because that was all very well and good as long as you were on the right side of the stream. She edged down the bank, hoping that she had chosen wisely.

As she picked her way along the shore, the sky turning pewter behind the black tree canopy, Ana thought about Mr. Peterson and his childhood friend floating their raft down this same stretch of water. How long had it taken them? Where had they camped?

What good had it done them, in the end?

———⚓———

"Howdy," said a voice through the trees.

Ana stopped. As the sun set, the shadows had begun to play tricks on her. Insects flitted and peeped in the brush, while the sound of the water seemed to echo the rustling of the branches.

About ten yards from where she stood, a woman sat surrounded by plastic shopping bags. Although the air was still soft and muggy, she wore a puffy vest over what looked like layers of clothing—cardigans, a high-necked work shirt—and thick, woolly socks curled over the tops of mud-splattered hiking boots. Her gray hair was piled in a knot at the top of her head, and her face was lined and white as the moon. "Got a light?" she said.

"No. Sorry."

"Want a brownie?" The woman held up a bag. "They're not the wacky-tabaccy kind. Some guy was doing a promotion outside the grocery store this afternoon. Fancy."

Against her better instincts, Ana stepped closer and reached into the bag. For a while now, her stomach had felt as if it was gnawing on itself. The brownies looked real. Tasted delicious.

"Take another one," said the woman. "I don't have anything to drink, but the water's pretty clean here and you can use one of my cups . . ."

"That's OK."

"Suit yourself." The woman took another brownie from the bag with quivering, nicotine-stained fingers. "'Way down, way down by the stream . . .'" she sang in a voice that was husky but in tune. She caught Ana's eye and smiled. "Do you know it? 'How very very sweet it would seem, once more just to dream, by the silvery moonlight . . .'"

"Vaguely."

"It's an old song. Kind of cheesy, I know."

They sat in silence for a few moments, and then the woman cocked a thumb over her shoulder.

"The viaduct's up that way. There's a guy on the corner with a hot dog stand. If you tell him Beth sent you, I bet he'll do you a frank for free."

"Really?" Ana glanced up the hill in relief. She hadn't realized civilization was so close by.

"You'll hear the cars from halfway up."

"Do you want anything? A hot dog?"

"I'm watching my figure." The woman winked. "You'd better hustle before it's totally dark. Nice meeting you . . . ?"

"Ana. Anneli."

"Anneli. That's pretty." The woman nodded. "You take care now."

After ten minutes, she recognized a street. Then another.

She was walking toward Mischa's house.

"What do you want to watch? We can download pretty much any-thing . . ." Mischa crossed his legs beneath him on his bed and began scrolling through options.

"I don't mind. Anything." Ana cupped the mug of tea in both hands, breathed in the soft lemon scent.

"Hey, here's that dude Sean was always going on about. Werner . . ."

"*Verner.* Werner Herzog."

"Uh-huh." Mischa clicked through to the summary. "*Fitzcarraldo.* About a guy obsessed with building an opera house in the jungle." He shrugged. "I can do business with that."

"Are you sure it's OK if I stay over tonight?"

"Yeah, of course. I'll take the futon. Just don't be surprised if you go down to the bathroom and find Mrs. Calder sitting in the hall-way—she does that sometimes. She's waiting for her cat to come in."

"OK." Ana leaned back against the headboard. "Thanks again. Really. I owe you."

"Stuff will work out. Don't worry."

Where does the soul come home to rest?
Who covereth it with protective wings?
Alas, the world offers no refuge to me
where sin cannot come, cannot contest.
No, no, no, no, here it is not,
The home of the soul is above in the light . . .

"You have a good voice," said Mischa, as they passed in the hallway outside the bathroom the next morning. He had a duvet and pillow bundled under one arm and had to crab-walk past her on the landing to squeeze by.

"I didn't know I was singing."

"Don't worry, it wasn't loud or anything. My parents are used to me practicing *Don Giovanni* in the shower."

"Opera," nodded Ana. "Suvi said."

"Suvi doesn't get it." Mischa shifted the pillow to his other arm. "She likes stuff with all the bells and whistles—you know, distortion and effects and that kind of thing. If there isn't a video to go with it, she's not really interested."

"I don't think she'd be into hymns," said Ana.

"You're probably right. But hey, any time you want to come to see one of our concerts . . ."

"That would be cool. Thanks."

"I was thinking . . . maybe one day I'll design theaters. Combine drawing with opera, you know? I could be like Fitzcarraldo, only less insane."

"Insane's OK. He got that ship over the mountain, didn't he?"

"Fair point. You have to dream big, I guess." Mischa tugged her braid with a wink. "Help yourself to whatever's in the fridge, OK?"

Her phone buzzed in her pocket, and Ana gestured thanks. She waited until he'd gone downstairs to flip open the screen.

———#———

Goo'ndach, read the text.
Suvi gave me your number. I hope that's OK.
Jonathan

———#———

She was pouring cereal into a bowl, still staring at his message, when the text came in from her mother.

Just let me know you're safe, it said. *Your father is beside himself.*

—⁂—

"For days after it happened, I'd wake up in the night to feel him sobbing in bed next to me," Lena said. "For all I know, that went on for weeks. Months."

They'd arranged to meet at the café at the far end of Mischa's street. Despite Suvi's talk about Mischa's parents buying a house in a fancy neighborhood, the main drag here was still pretty shabby: dollar stores and secondhand shops dotted between greasy spoons and dive bars. Block by block, the street smells ebbed between Indian food and torn garbage bags, a plastic scent from the wig store and something bodily and stale outside the community housing. "You didn't hang around to find out," she said.

Lena ignored the note of accusation in Ana's voice and stirred her coffee with an unreadable expression. She hadn't bothered to put on any makeup before coming out to meet Ana. Without the faintest slick of mascara, her eyelashes looked pale and brittle. Even the freckles that dotted her cheekbones looked faded, drained of life.

"He spent the nights begging God to forgive him," she said quietly. "The days were a different matter. He withdrew from everyone. Me and you, especially. It was as if he was afraid to be near us."

—⁂—

"You don't have to believe me," she continued. "You don't have to care or try to understand. But someone has to say this for him. *It nearly killed him, Ani.* The guilt. He wasn't afraid for himself, but for us. After the police came—"

"So they did come? At the time?"

Outside, an elderly woman in a pink nightgown and knee socks shuffled down the sidewalk, singing loudly. A plastic tiara had been stabbed into her riot of frizzy white hair, red circles drawn in lipstick on her sallow cheeks. Ana watched her go before fixing her gaze back on Lena.

"A man came up the drive one day, claiming to be lost," Lena said. "His car had broken down. He was Guaraní. I was hanging out some washing. I said I'd get one of the men to help, but he insisted he didn't want to be any trouble. He just wanted to know if I knew the route to Moth, if I could confirm that there was a truck that came up to us once or twice a week for shipments, because if there was he was hoping he could hitch a ride home with them later in the day. I felt sorry for him. He didn't look like a policeman. I didn't think. I said yes . . ."

"And he was a cop?"

"I don't know. He was working for them, anyway. They turned up the next day, asking questions. They insisted on interrogating me, but before I went in Gerhard Buhler had something to say. Years before, before he married Rachael, before Maria and Susanna were born, Gerhard had . . . he'd been interested in me, shall we say." Lena avoided meeting Ana's eye. "There were threats. I could see the writing on the wall: Gerhard was going to punish me for spurning him all those years ago by turning my husband over to the police. He was going to ruin Miloh and make pariahs of you and me. So I fled. At first, with you—but I've told you that already . . ."

Her mother pressed her fists to her eyes, rubbed hard. When she looked up again, the skin was white and startled.

"He doesn't want your pity, Ana," she said in a small voice. "He's punished himself enough already. He knows he has to let you go. But don't do what I did. He doesn't deserve that all over again."

—#—

He was sitting on her bed when she came in, an enormous book open on his lap. *The Complete Works of Shakespeare.*

"Will you take it with you?" he said, without looking up. "Back to her? I never was able to make head or tail of it."

All that way, Ana thought. They traveled all that way, to the very edge of the continent, to escape from the rest of the world. To make a better life, to live with dignity, in peace. And still, all that way from the rest of civilization, trouble found him. It didn't seem fair.

Ana closed the book and set it on the bed. Climbed onto her father's lap and circled her arms around his neck. Tight, tight, to still the shuddering shoulders, to silence the sobs of a little boy stuck, alone, at the farthest branch in the *tipu* tree.

—*#*—

I'd like to be able to say that I eventually got a letter from Susanna that answered all my questions, tied up the loose ends. I've written a letter to her, not saying too much about Mama and Papa for fear of getting Papa into trouble, just letting her know that I'm safe and happy and that I miss her and Justina and I hope that Maria and the baby are doing OK. I told her how it took coming here for me to see what had been in front of me all along in Colony Felicidad, to see all the things that had been kept from me as a child. I suppose, sometimes, you only get to properly understand a place by leaving it.

That's what Lena said the evening I moved in with her for good, as we poured over atlases borrowed from the library. She loved the pictures: the mountain ranges, lakes, seas, islands and arbitrary man-made borders. But I was awed by the index: so many places, most of them so small and never to be imagined, let alone visited. Neatly ordered by alphabetical standing, stripped of history and context, the mundane listed side by side with the unpronounceable.

Every one of them was home to someone. A place left behind, and returned to.

So, here we are: sitting at the airport with a stack of magazines on the seat between us, breaking a bar of Cadbury Fruit & Nut and waiting for our gate to be called. Lena is using her teeth to snap the tag off the sunglasses she bought in Duty Free, and I'm looking out the big glass wall at the expanse of concrete hangars and landing strips, and the distant cluster of buildings beyond them that is downtown.

I've promised to bring back an alpaca wool scarf for Suvi. Mischa just wants a postcard from Machu Picchu. I told him I didn't know if there was a post office actually *in* Machu Picchu, but that I'd do my best. I've told Jonathan that it's fine that Suvi gave him my phone number. I pretended to be annoyed with her for about three minutes, but she could clearly tell I didn't mean it. She even suggested that I send him a postcard too. I told her to mind her own business for once.

I'll send one to Papa, though. He's staying with Johan and Katherina in Aylmer for the time being. Apparently Elizabeth's cat is expecting another litter in a few weeks. She's promised me one of the kittens when I get back. I've already decided to call it Papillon.

The screen above our heads flickers into life, and a voice over the intercom announces our gate. We shove the magazines into a plastic bag and steer our suitcases around the ankles of people still waiting for their flights. My stomach does a weird fluttery thing, and then Lena stops and turns to look at me.

"Did you just get that?" she said. "That starting a journey feeling? Kind of excited, but also kind of scared?"

"Yeah."

She slings her handbag over her shoulder and takes my hand.

"Inca Trail, here we come," she says.

Acknowledgements

Many thanks to Damaris Schmucker, Kerry Fast and Anna Wall for their generosity and honesty in advising on the Mennonite experience in Canada and abroad; to Leila Rasheed for her perceptive and instrumental feedback on an early draft; and to Tara Walker, Samantha Swenson and all the team at Tundra Books for helping to bring this story to fruition with unfailing enthusiasm, patience and humour.

The author would like to thank the Ontario Arts Council for providing funding support during the completion of this work.

Other People's Words